No Castanets at the Wells

Lorna Hill wrote her first stories in an exercise book after watching Pavlova dance in Newcastle. Her daughter, Vicki, aged ten, discovered one of these stories and was so delighted by it that Lorna Hill wrote several more and soon they were published. Vicki trained as a ballet dancer at Sadler's Wells and from her letters, Mrs Hill was able to glean the knowledge which forms the background for the 'Wells' stories.

No Castanets At The Wells, the third book in the series, is about another of Veronica's relations, Caroline, who goes to the Ballet School but discovers that her affinity is for Spanish dancing rather than classical ballet. She gets the chance to dance with Angelo, a friend of Sebastian's and after a hectic BBC audition, Angelo and Caroline team up.

A Dream of Sadler's Wells, *Veronica At The Wells* and *Masquerade At The Wells* are also published in Piccolo.

By the same author in Piccolo Books

A DREAM OF SADLER'S WELLS
VERONICA AT THE WELLS
MASQUERADE AT THE WELLS

No Castanets at the Wells

LORNA HILL

Illustrated by Kathleen Whapham

A Piccolo Book

PAN BOOKS LTD
LONDON

First published 1953 by Evans Brothers Ltd.
This edition published 1972 by Pan Books Ltd,
33 Tothill Street, London, S.W.1

ISBN 0 330 02899 5

Printed in Great Britain by
Richard Clay (The Chaucer Press), Ltd, Bungay, Suffolk

To all the children who have written to me
begging me to 'write more about Sebastian,
Veronica, and the rest of them'

Contents

THE FIRST YEAR

Winter

Summer

THE SECOND YEAR

Winter

Summer

THE THIRD YEAR

Winter

Summer

The First Year

Winter

Chapter 1

Nothing Much Happens

I'VE often thought I'd like to write a story – I mean a story about myself – but the trouble is where to begin.

'At the beginning, of course,' I can hear you say. Yes, but where exactly *is* the beginning? Some people might say it was long, long ago on that July day when my cousin, Veronica, came to live with us all at Bracken Hall, because it was Veronica who first showed me how lovely dancing is, and made me want to dance, too. Other people might, say 'Caroline Scott, be honest with yourself. You never really thought about dancing seriously until you met Angelo and heard him play his castanets; now did you?' Well, no, I suppose I didn't. As a matter of fact, I had always intended to take up domestic science when I left school and learn to cook nice things for other people to eat. Mummy still thought I was going to do that on the day when *I* think it all began – that is, on the Monday after Veronica went back to London to seize her chance to get a part in the ballet *Job*. You see, Sebastian, Fiona, and I were left behind to spend the rest of the holidays without her. Sebastian is my cousin, too – on Daddy's side – and Fiona is my elder sister. Sebastian always calls Veronica his 'cousin-sort-of', but she's really no relation to him at all, only to Fiona and me.

It was awful without Veronica. For one thing, we were

practically snowed up, so Sebastian couldn't get into Newcastle to practise with his beloved Musical Society, because every time the men got the road dug out, another fall of snow would come during the night and block us in again. Added to this was the fact that, in the heat of the moment, Veronica had forgotten all about his concert and gone hareing off to London without as much as a backward glance. At any rate, this is how Sebastian put it. No wonder he was in a filthy temper! For the past two days he'd gone about with a set look upon his face, and it was as much as your life was worth even to speak to him, let alone to ask him to ride with you on the snowy moors. Fiona wouldn't go out, either, because she got chilblains and the cold made her nose red, and Trixie said that the house was the right place for Christian folk in such weather, and why people wanted to go tramping about outside – floundering in snowdrifts, slipping into frozen burns, and getting showers of snow on their heads every time the wind blew it off the branches – she didn't know.

'If Miss Veronica was here, *she'd* have gone out with you, I shouldn't wonder,' she added. 'I never knew a child so fond of wandering about the countryside in all weathers!'

'Yes, but Veronica *isn't* here,' I argued. 'And Fiona's afraid of her nose – I mean, afraid it'll turn red for the New Year party at the Frazers, and Sebastian won't go *anywhere*. He just sits at the piano all day long, playing somebody's Dead March. Oh, Trixie, *do* come down to the lake, *please*, Trixie. Somebody said the ice was hard enough for skating.'

But Trixie wouldn't. She said she'd go through fire and water for her bairns – meaning Fiona and me – but be frozen to the marrow she wouldn't.

'Anyway, it's nearly time for your supper, Miss Caroline,' she put in quite unnecessarily, because I'd been given a wrist-watch from Mummy and Daddy at Christmas, so I knew the time as well as she did. 'You ought to be off to bed early tonight, you know, after all the late nights you've had over Christmas – Master Sebastian's concert, and that.'

I hastily withdrew from the kitchen before any more references were made to going to bed early. I put on my Wellingtons, wrapped a woolly scarf round my ears, and set off for the lake by myself.

The long drive was like fairyland. Overhead the interlacing boughs were loaded with frozen snow which glittered in the frosty moonlight. The air was so still and cold that it almost hurt you to breathe. The snowy path squeaked underfoot, and there was a faint singing in the air that meant the thermometer was down to several degrees below zero. In the distance I could see the lodge at the bottom of the drive where Sebastian lived. The lighted window of Uncle Adrian's study glowed warmly out of the winter twilight. I wondered if Sebastian was inside, flung moodily down in the depths of an easy chair, or idly turning over the pages of some musician's life – Chopin, most likely, or perhaps Tchaikovsky. Ballet, anyway. Or maybe he'd be writing music – something very sad and gloomy. I couldn't help knowing that Sebastian was an exceedingly strange boy. Especially strange he'd been of late – in fact, ever since Veronica came home for the Christmas holidays. Sometimes I felt he actually disliked Veronica, but at other times I knew in my heart that he was terribly fond of her. It was very puzzling, and not very comfortable, because you never knew what to say, and whatever you said it seemed to be the wrong thing!

I left Sebastian's cottage behind me and made my way along the path towards the lake. It wasn't easy because the bushes on both sides were bent under their burden of snow, until they almost met across the path. I got pretty wet forcing my way through them. But when I reached the lake, it was certainly worth a wetting. The stretch of frozen water lay before me like a shining mirror of silver. The fir trees round its banks stood motionless, like enchanted princesses under a spell. The little beach, where we bathed in summer, lay there, a half-moon of dazzling white, unblemished by a single footprint. The star-studded sky hung above me like a jewelled bowl.

For a moment I stood there, quite still. It was like being in some strange fairyland whose shore had never been crossed by mortal footstep. Then a faint 'Coo-ee! Co-ee!' came from the far side of the lake, and I knew that someone else had felt compelled to venture out into the snowy moonlight.

'Co-ee! Co-ee!' I called back. 'Is that you, Sebastian?'

'Yes, it's me. What are you doing here, Caroline?'

'Nothing much,' I answered. 'As a matter of fact, I was *thinking*.'

There was a rustle, a tinkle of ice falling on ice, the snowy bushes parted, and Sebastian stood before me – the old, happy Sebastian, his mouth lifted at the corners, his blue eyes snapping.

'Thinking, Caroline?' he said in mock amazement. 'Whatever possessed you to do that? Why, you might break something!'

'If you want to know,' I said, 'I was thinking how like one of Veronica's ballets this is.' I motioned towards the frozen lake. 'I forget the name of it.'

'*Les Patineurs,*' said Sebastian promptly. 'The one about skating. It goes like this—' He shot off across the ice, humming the haunting music of the ballet.

'Do be careful, Sebastian!' I warned. 'The ice may not be hard enough to bear you, and anyway you ought to have skates on to do that.'

'I *shall* have skates on soon,' laughed Sebastian, coming back to me. 'I mean to skate here with Angelo.'

'Angelo?' I repeated. 'Who is Angelo?'

'Friend of mine,' Sebastian said casually. 'He's coming to lunch the day after tomorrow.'

'Well, I do think you might have told me,' I grumbled.

'I *have* told you, haven't I?' Sebastian said. 'Anyway, I didn't know myself until last night after the concert. Angelo plays the flute, and he's dead keen on the Musical Society.

Queer chap, Angelo. I never know whether he's keener on music or dancing. Sometimes I think dancing has it.'

'Oh!' I said rather flatly. I had never met a boy who was a dancer, and I wasn't quite sure that I liked the idea.

'You needn't say "Oh!" like that,' teased Sebastian. 'Angelo isn't at all pretty-pretty, if that's what you're thinking. I mean, he doesn't go in for ballet dancing. Says he can't stand it! Says it's sissy! He's wrong, of course, but it's no use arguing with Angelo.'

'Well, what sort of dancing does he do, then, if he isn't a ballet dancer?' I asked. 'Tap dancing – like Fred Astaire?'

'Not likely!'

'Well, what sort, then?'

'Wait and see, as somebody said to somebody, I forget who,' said Sebastian. 'One of those poetical johnnies, I expect.'

'Oh, it doesn't really matter,' I retorted loftily. 'I don't expect I shall see much of your precious Angelo, or whatever his funny name is. It isn't as if he *lived* here.'

'That's where you're wrong,' answered Sebastian. 'It's on the cards he *may* live here.'

'What?' I echoed. 'You mean with you? In your cottage?'

'No, not with me exactly,' explained Sebastian patiently. 'There wouldn't be room. But you see, after my concert, I had a talk with a man called Messenger – Humphrey Messenger. I don't expect you've heard of him, but he's no end of a swell in the music world. Got a lot of influence, of course. Well, he seemed to think I wasn't too bad. In short, he said it was about time I moved on to the Royal College of Music.'

'Oh *Sebastian*!' I wailed. 'Not you as well as Veronica!'

'Keep your hair on! I shan't be going for a bit yet,' Sebastian assured me. 'Probably not till May. And anyway, when I do go, you'll have Angelo in my place to keep you in order. Much more exciting, I can tell you!' Then, as I still looked puzzled, he relented and explained further. 'You see, when I go to London, my room will be going begging, so Father and I thought Angelo might like it. He's coming to Durham University to study music, and living in lodgings isn't very inspiring and the hostel is full up. By the way, Angelo's father happens to be one of *my* father's best friends. So, all things considered, we thought it would be a good idea if Angelo came to live here.'

'Then he isn't Italian?' I said. 'I thought all Angelos were Italian.'

'No, as a matter of fact, he's Spanish – Spanish to the core. His father's name is Ibañez, and his people own a huge hotel in Harrogate.'

'Can he speak English?' I asked, running my fingernail down the surface of the boathouse window and watching the icy flakes glittering in the moonlight. 'Because if he can't, we shan't get on very far. All the Spanish I know is *grazie*, and that's because it was in a play we once did at school. And now I come to think of it, I believe *grazie* is Italian, not Spanish.'

Sebastian laughed.

'You're right – it is! But you needn't worry – Angelo can speak English nearly as well as you can yourself. In fact, you'd never know he wasn't English until—' He stopped suddenly.

'Until what?'

'I was going to say until he dances,' said Sebastian. '*Then* you know he's Spanish to the backbone!'

'Oh, then I suppose he does Spanish dancing?'

'Right first time! Toreador, Carmen, and all that stuff.' Sebastian broke off a snow-encrusted twig, thrust it between his teeth, struck an attitude, and took a step or two on the frozen sand. Then he stopped and hastily removed the twig.

'Gosh! It's cold. Makes my teeth ache! I think it's time I was making tracks for home. It's getting late, and I feel like turning in early after last night.'

'That's what Trixie said,' I told him. 'It's funny, Sebastian, but your father lets you go to bed any old time you like. I don't suppose he'd worry if you sat up all night, so—'

'So, of course, I toddle off early if I feel tired,' said Sebastian. 'That's human nature all over! You and Fiona are shooed about by old Trixie like a couple of chickens by a mother hen, and the consequence is, the later you stay up the more of a treat it is. By the way, I'll see you home before I hop off.'

'Oh, you needn't bother,' I assured him. 'It's as light as day with the full moon.' I looked up at the golden disc sailing in an almost cloudless sky.

'All the same, I'll come,' insisted Sebastian. 'Always the little gentleman, yours truly! *Toujours la politesse.* "Take your turn in the queue!" as the executioner said to the aristocrats in the French Revolution when he cut off their heads. Some bold, bad robber might run off with you, Caroline. What a shock he'd get though, if he did. I have an idea he'd return you by the next post labelled: "Unsuitable for a pet. This variety bites!"'

I couldn't help giggling. Sebastian was very funny when he was in a mood like this. It was really hard to believe he was the same person as the moody boy I'd seen only this morning.

We walked back along the path in single file, and then over the snow lawns towards the house. There it lay, Bracken Hall, my home. By right it was really Sebastian's, I told myself. His father was the eldest son, and it was just bad luck that Uncle Adrian hadn't got enough money to live in his ancestral home, whereas Daddy had made lots in trade, and so was able to keep Bracken Hall in the Scott family.

'Sebastian?' I said suddenly.

'Yes, what, Caroline?'

'Sebastian – do you *mind* not being able to live in your ancestral home?' I asked him.

He turned away from me so that I could only see his profile, black and proud against the pale evening sky.

'What, me?' he said mockingly. 'My good girl, now what on earth should I want to live in *that* place for?' He made a dramatic gesture towards the lighted house. 'Too many rooms – far too draughty – old-fashioned – just a blessed white elephant! Give me a cottage every time. It's a lot warmer, for one thing.'

But although he joked about it, and pretended he didn't care, I knew in my heart that Sebastian loved his real home passionately, but he was far too proud to admit it.

'Don't grown-up people look funny when they're doing things and you can't hear them talking?' I said, mainly to change the subject which I felt was a painful one to Sebastian. 'Especially when they don't know you're watching them. Look at Mummy passing the coffee round. She looks terribly bored!'

'And Uncle John is fast asleep with his mouth open. He looks exactly like a cod-fish!' laughed Sebastian. 'Pardon my rude remarks about your father, Caroline, but it's the truth! Gosh! That wakened him up all right, Aunt June asking him if he wanted sugar in his coffee. And look at old Trixie! She's asking them if they've seen you, I shouldn't wonder. She looks quite worried.'

'Yes, I must dash!' I laughed. 'Poor Trixie! I expect she thinks I've been swallowed by a snowdrift! Thank you for coming with me, Sebastian. See you tomorrow, I expect.' With that I left him standing on the edge of the lawn and ran towards the entrance. The ornamental tubs at the top of the steps stood sentinel, like twin snowmen, and on the head of each was a fat, white cushion of snow. It seemed a shame to walk up the steps and spoil their virgin whiteness.

'Oh, the winter is lovely!' I said to myself. 'At least, it's beautiful here in Northumberland, though I expect it's awful if you have to live in London. Poor Veronica! She must be frightfully keen on dancing to leave all this and go back to Mrs Crapper's dingy boarding house and her ballet school.'

'Miss Caroline! Miss Caroline! Where are you?' came Trixie's voice from the french window of the lounge.

'Coming, Trixie!' I yelled back.

In another moment I had reached her.

'Shut the window quickly, Miss Caroline, do!' Trixie said with a shiver. 'You're letting all the cold air come into the house.' She fussed around me like an old hen, as Sebastian would have said, drawing the velvet curtains closely over the long windows, and effectively shutting out the lovely snowy landscape and the star-spangled sky. I couldn't help sighing. It was so much more beautiful out in the snow than in the warm and curtained house.

Chapter 2

I Get a Letter from Veronica

THE next morning was Monday. I was down bright and early to see if there were any letters for me. I got to the kitchen door just as old Billy, the postman, arrived. Sarah bustled to meet him – Sarah is our cook, and she is Northumbrian to the backbone, with an accent you could cut with a knife.

'Come awa in, man!' she said in her warm, Northumbrian voice. 'Ye'll tak a cup o' tae to warm yesel' up a bit?'

'Oh, aye,' answered Billy, dumping down his bag on the kitchen floor, and shaking himself like a dog. 'There's a rare nip i' the air, the marnin'. There's twa letters and a wee parcel for your mother, Miss Caroline,' he added, turning to me. 'Oh, aye – and a tidy few for your pa.'

'You're sure there isn't a letter for me, Billy?' I asked anxiously. 'I'm expecting one.'

Billy warmed his hands round the basin-sized cup provided by Sarah, and winked solemnly at nobody in particular.

'I'll look in me bag in a wee while, and maybe I'll find one,' he said offhandedly.

'Oh, Billy, look *now*!' I pleaded. 'Couldn't you look *now*! You don't know how much I'm wanting a letter. It – it might be from Veronica – my cousin, you know.'

'Oh, aye,' Billy said, putting down the cup and rummaging once more in his bag. 'I mind your cousin weel. A real decent bit lassie, with no lardy-dardy ways aboot her. A bonny wee lassie, too. And look what I have here, Miss Caroline – a letter for ye, after aal, and me nearly forgettin' it! It's got the London postmark on it, an' aal.'

'It's from Veronica!' I yelled. 'Oh, *thank* you, Billy!' I felt nearly as grateful to old Billy as if he had written it himself.

And indeed I had something to be grateful for. It was no joke, as I well knew, struggling through snowdrifts, ploughing through snowy fields and over frozen roads with the country mail, and old Billy was not as young as he had been.

'Well, I'll be on me way,' he said to Sarah. 'And thank ye kindly for the tea. It'll keep the cald wind oot.' So saying, he shouldered his bag once more, and set off into the snowy morning.

I dashed upstairs to read Veronica's letter. Fortunately, there was no one in the bathroom, so I locked myself in there, and then tore open the envelope. I expect you'll be thinking that the bathroom was an odd place in which to read one's letters, but I can assure you it was a lot more comfortable than my bedroom, which resembled nothing so much as the North Pole at the present moment. You see, what with the cost of living going up and up, and coke and electricity being so expensive, we weren't as well off as we had been when we'd first come to Bracken Hall. Quite by accident I'd heard Mummy and Daddy talking about it just before Christmas, which was the time when we usually turned on all the central heating. Daddy was saying that we simply *must* economize somewhere, and why not on the heating? Mummy had shrugged her shoulders and said she supposed that was as good as anything. So the central heating hadn't been turned on at all this winter, the downstairs rooms only being supplied with electric heating. The lounge had a novel affair that flickered and made you think there was a lovely fire in the room, whereas really there was no heat at all. Sebastian called it a 'ghastly swindle'!

But to go back to my letter.

> Dear Caroline [it said]. I was going to ring up on Saturday night on the cheap rate and say I'd arrived safely, but the rehearsal went on and on, and by the time I'd got back to Mrs Crapper's, I realized that you'd all be at Sebastian's concert. I tried to get through at six o'clock tonight, but they said your phone was out of order. I expect it was the

snowstorm. Anyway, would you please apologize to Aunt June for me, and tell her it wasn't that I forgot. I shall try to catch the last post tonight so that you'll get this letter early tomorrow morning.

To go back to the beginning. I arrived at King's Cross at the usual unholy hour of 5.30 or thereabouts, and stayed in the train till seven. I didn't want to go waking up poor old Martha at that time in the morning.

I felt very lonely, not having anyone to meet me, and I couldn't help remembering that other time when Sebastian saw me off at Newcastle and Jonathan met me on the platform here. But of course it couldn't he helped. Jonathan is still in Northumberland, and Sebastian – of course Sebastian is still furious with me.

To speak of happier things, the rehearsal went off splendidly. Going to Covent Garden in the Tube I was all in a daydream, and if it hadn't been for a young man nudging my arm and saying: 'This is where you get off, young lady, isn't it?' I'd have passed my station. I was most awfully grateful, because it would have been awful to be late for one's very first rehearsal, wouldn't it? I told the young man so, and he laughed like anything and said I'd be wiser later on – rehearsals were always at least an hour late in starting. He was a very good-looking young man with almond-shaped eyes that gave him a fawn-like appearance, and I felt somehow that he was vaguely familiar. Imagine my astonishment when two girls from the Wells School who happened to have seen me talking to him said in awestruck voices: '*Veronica!* What did he say to you?'

'What did *who* say?' I asked.

'Josef Linsk. The young man you were talking to.'

I nearly fell flat on the station platform.

'You don't mean to say that was Josef Linsk,' I said. 'The famous dancer? The young man who's dancing Elihu in *Job*, the ballet I'm to be a Son of the Morning in. At least, I'm *hoping* to be one.'

'Why, of course it was!' they laughed. 'Really, Veronica, you *are* a dreamer! You're always talking to people and not knowing who they are! First it was Oscar Deveraux, the ballet critic, and then Irma Foster—'

'I didn't talk to them,' I declared. 'I only wished I had!'

But all the same, Caroline, there's a lot of truth in what Dorothy and Phyllis said. I do seem to go into daydreams and get people all wrong. I couldn't help thinking about the very first day I met Sebastian – my taking him for the gardener's boy, and asking him if he was just off to hoe the onions!

But to get back to the rehearsal. It went off quite well. Madame showed us our positions as Sons of the Morning on a miniature 'set' of steps, just like the real stage. She explained the music, too – it's Vaughan Williams' music, you know, and terribly difficult. I feel I didn't do too badly. Anyway, I've got the part, and I'm in the Farendole in *The Sleeping Beauty*, too.

It was lovely to be dancing with Toni again. Honestly, Caroline, he's so *sweet*. You've no idea what a help he was, explaining things to me. You see, all the others knew the dance, and it was pretty hair-raising, being pitched head first into the middle of it, without knowing in the least what it was all about. But, as Toni says, as long as you don't look strained, and do everything with an air, nobody minds. As a matter of fact, the audience is far too busy watching the principals to notice what the mere members of the *corps de ballet* do. Well, whether this is so or not, it made me feel a lot better, and I threw myself into the dance without getting into too flat a spin. Sorry! This seems to be a totally unintended pun!

I saw Josef Linsk again after the rehearsal, and he actually gave me a funny little bow – he's foreign, you know. Hungarian, I think. I saw Robert Helpmann, too. He's guest artist for the season. He's a magnificent dancer, and to see him as Satan was an experience one can't easily forget. He looks so pagan, so wicked, and yet in a way, noble – all at the same time. It's difficult to explain how a person can be all these things at once, but I assure you Helpmann manages it!

Belinda – you remember I told you about her? – she was at the school with me before she joined the Company – well, she was one of Job's daughters. She's a brilliant dancer, too, but there's just *something* about her that spoils her. It's hard to explain this, as well, but I think it's because she hasn't got a nice mind. Anyway, I didn't like watching her very much. I wouldn't say this to anyone but you, Caroline, because people might say I was jealous!

Well, now I think I've told you all the news. It's queer to think of Bracken Hall amongst its snowy woods – so cold and silent, and the moors piled up with drifts higher than your head. Here it's just cold and dirty! Yet I love London, too, and that's something else that's hard to explain.

Before I finish this letter, I want to ask you to do something for me, Caroline. Could you find out if Sebastian is still furious with me? If you think he'd listen, would you explain that it wasn't that I forgot his concert, really. It was there all the time at the back of my mind. Truly it was! It was only the shock of the telegram that made everything go right out of my head for the time being. I'm pretty sure it would have done the same to him. Think of it – the chance I'd been waiting for all my life; the chance of being in one of Madame's own ballets! But I wouldn't have hurt Sebastian's feelings for the world. Why, he's one of my very greatest friends. If it hadn't been for Sebastian, as you know, I'd have run away from you all at Bracken Hall the very first morning. And as a matter of fact I'd never have got to my audition for the Wells at all if it hadn't been for him. I just hate to think of Sebastian angry with me.

After the rehearsal, I kept thinking about the concert and wondering how it had gone. You don't know how much I longed to hear Sebastian's *Woodland Symphony*. But you see, when you're a professional dancer, you've got to put your profession first, no matter what your private feelings are. Surely Sebastian must know that – why, he's going to be professional himself. Please, *please*, Caroline – couldn't you explain to him how it was with me, and perhaps now, when he's not quite so angry with me, he'll listen to you.

Much love to you all,

VERONICA

PS – I wonder if Perkins got home all right in all that snow? I was frightfully worried about him, and all the time I was in the train I kept thinking of him stuck in a snow-drift, and me not there to help him dig himself out. Please will you thank him again for getting me to the station in time to catch the train, and give him my love. Really, although I know Sebastian hates Perkins, *I* think he's an awfully nice man. Sometimes I think Sebastian just hates people because they've got big ears, or sticking-out teeth, or something quite unreasonable like that. I wonder if that's being temperamental? Sebastian called *me* temperamental once, I remember. Personally, I think he's even more so!

Love again,

VERONICA

I read the letter over twice, and then put it into my pocket with a sigh. It was Veronica's request about Sebastian that worried me. It was going to be awfully difficult to act as intermediary between the two of them. Quite frankly I didn't know how to set about it. If you as much as mentioned Veronica's name, Sebastian would fling himself off in a temper. Or he'd say: 'Oh, shut up, Caroline! Let's forget about Veronica!' And what could you do in these circumstances? You couldn't very well run after him and *order* him to listen to you, and in any case, I reflected, Sebastian never did things when you ordered him to do them.

I unlocked the bathroom door, and went slowly down to

breakfast. Trixie met me outside the schoolroom door and wanted to know if I had toothache.

'You look so solemn, Miss Caroline,' she remarked when I said I hadn't. 'It's not often you haven't a smile for me in the morning. You're quite sure you feel well?'

'Quite well, thank you, Trixie,' I told her, grinning broadly to reassure her, though I didn't feel a bit like grinning, really. 'It's just that I've had a letter from Veronica, and she wants me to do something – well, something rather difficult.'

Fiona looked up from her grapefruit – she wouldn't have porridge, even in the winter, in case it made her fat.

'Oh, I suppose she wrote pages and pages all about her stupid ballet,' she scoffed. 'I expect she wanted you to help her to make some of her costumes?'

'You don't make your own costumes in the proper ballet,' I told her. 'They're all made for you by famous theatrical costume designers, and all you have to do is put them on and look beautiful.'

I'm afraid I knew this would annoy Fiona. She liked having masses of new clothes, and I must admit that she usually succeeded in looking beautiful in them.

'Personally, I can't imagine Veronica looking beautiful in anything,' she retorted. 'She's far too pale and skinny.'

'She's just right for the ballet,' I said, calmly helping myself to sugar and cream. 'You've got to be slim for ballet. It wouldn't do if Veronica was at fat as you are.'

Fiona pushed her empty plate away from her so vigorously that she almost upset the cream jug into my lap.

'Or you,' she said sweetly.

Of course, I had asked for it, but her words hurt just the same. There was a great deal too much truth in it. I *was* far too fat.

'Trixie,' I said suddenly, 'I've made up my mind. Fiona's quite right. I *am* as fat as a pig! I'm going to slim straight away.'

Poor Trixie was horrified.

'You'll do no such thing, Miss Caroline,' she said. 'Miss Fiona, you're a very naughty girl to say such things. If you *are* a little on the plump side, Miss Caroline, it's nothing but puppy fat. You'll slim down in a year or two, see if you don't.'

'Yes, but I'm not going to wait for a year or two,' I said firmly. 'I want to be slim *now*. I'm not going to have sugar in my tea, and I'm not going to eat any more cream cakes or rich pastries, like they say you shouldn't on the wireless. I'm going to be a martyr to my figure from now on! Oh, and another thing – I asked Mummy if I might leave Miss Gilchrist and go to Veronica's dancing school, Miss Martin's. She said I might, and I'm going to her next week. That ought to help my slimming. You've got to work awfully hard at Miss Martin's, Veronica says.'

'Mummy has arranged for me to have ballet lessons next term at school,' Fiona said, her nose in the air. 'They cost the earth, so I expect they'll be an awful lot better than your stupid Miss Martin's.'

'I expect they won't,' I snapped. 'Nobody could be better than Miss Martin, and, as a matter of fact, money has nothing whatever to do with it. Sometimes the most expensive dancing schools are the awfullest. Gilbert says so.'

'Gilbert?' echoed Fiona superciliously.

'Mr Delahaye,' I explained. 'He's one of the instructors at the Wells, and Veronica says he's perfectly marvellous. Well, if *he* says Miss Martin's good, she must be.'

Poor Trixie hadn't been able to get a word in edgeways all this time.

'I do wish you two children would stop bickering,' she said as soon as there was a pause. 'Why you can't eat your breakfast without quarrelling beats me.'

'Fiona began it,' I declared. 'Sneering at Veronica's letter! And, by the way—' I stopped short suddenly. The mention of the letter had reminded me of Veronica's request.

'By the way *what*?' snapped Fiona.

'Oh, nothing,' I answered. But, as a matter of fact, I had

just at that moment made up my mind. I would show Sebastian Veronica's letter. Then he wouldn't be able to walk away before I'd begun to explain. Also I felt that Veronica had put the matter much better than I ever could.

After breakfast I put on Wellingtons and coat, and set off down the drive towards Sebastian's cottage, followed by Fiona's warning: 'Don't forget we're going to Hexham before lunch. I have an appointment at the hairdresser's at eleven. The road's open at last, but it's still pretty rough and Perkins says we must start not a minute after ten.'

'Oh, all right,' I shouted back. I couldn't help feeling it was an awful waste having to go into a town – even a little one like Hexham – on a lovely, glittering blue-and-white morning like this, but I supposed it was all part of the penalty of being grown up, like Fiona who's nearly sixteen. The trouble was *I* had to suffer for it, too, because Mummy had said I might as well have my hair washed and trimmed, as well, while Fiona was having hers 'set'.

'Sebastian! Sebastian!' I shouted as I neared the pretty cottage at the bottom of the drive where Sebastian lived. 'Co-ee! Sebastian!'

There was no answer, so I knocked at the blue door, and stood waiting. The trees on either side of the drive were mostly firs. They stood motionless, like Christmas trees, each branch bearing its decoration, not of glass toys, but of crisp snow, glittering in the cold winter sunshine. The sky was very blue and clear. In the nearby shrubbery two thrushes began to quarrel, their harsh, metallic cries destroying the almost unearthly stillness.

'Sebastian!' I yelled again.

Still no answer.

I left the front door, and made my way round to the back of the house, nearly colliding with Bella McIntosh who 'does' for Uncle Adrian and Sebastian during the daytime. She sleeps in the village. Bella was carrying a zinc bowl in one hand and two brown eggs, held very carefully, in the other.

'Oh, hullo, Bella!' I said. 'I wondered where you were. I thought perhaps you'd be feeding the hens.'

'My word, Miss Caroline,' Bella said, her round, good-natured face redder than usual after her exertions, 'you did give me a start! Them hens tak a deal o' looking after i' the cold weather. They do, an' all! It's half a dozen hands ye need to feed 'em wi mash, scatter corn for 'em, gi' 'em water and dig 'em oot! It's a octy-puss ye have to be!'

'I expect it *is* rather a job,' I agreed, trying not to laugh. 'Can I help, Bella?'

'It's a' finished noo,' Bella assured me. 'But thank ye kindly, Miss Caroline, for thinkin' aboot it. Ye're a canny bit bairn! To tell ye the truth, Master Sabestian dug 'em oot for us afore he went oot on his pony.'

'Oh, Sebastian's out riding?' I said. 'I wondered why he wasn't somewhere about. You don't know where he's gone, do you, Bella?'

Bella shook her head.

'A canna say, Miss Caroline. He did mention summat aboot gannen doon tae the shoe-macker i' the village for some shoes he wanted for his concert, but why he couldna gan i' his brogues a dinna ken.'

'Oh, it would be his *evening* shoes,' I laughed. 'Most important to have the proper kind. Sebastian would think so, anyway! It's a nuisance he's out, though. I wanted to see him most particularly.'

I followed Bella inside the cottage, and wandered into the lounge. It was pleasantly untidy; in fact a typically masculine room. Sebastian's music covered the piano, and overflowed on to several chairs, as well. Uncle Adrian had evidently been planning the summer holiday, for there were a couple of ordnance-survey maps of the Highlands of Scotland spread out on the floor, and a guidebook of the island of Skye open on the table. There was a lovely smell of leather, tobacco, and new paper – the latter due, I expect, to a pile of new music reposing on the floor by the window. It had evidently just come by post.

Although I had hoped to find Sebastian at home so that I could explain about the letter, it was rather a relief that he wasn't there. If he flew into a temper at the mere mention of Veronica's name, as he had a habit of doing, at least I shouldn't be there to see it!

I picked up a sheet of manuscript paper and wrote:

> Dear Sebastian,
>
> Veronica asked me to tell you how it was about her missing your concert, but I'm sure she's explained ever so much better than I could, so I am leaving her letter for you to read. *Please* read it, Sebastian. Poor Veronica! You can see for yourself how miserable she is.
>
> Sorry to miss you. Will see you later – have got to go to the hairdresser's now, worse luck!
>
> CAROLINE

I propped the letter up on the music-rest and shut the door of the lounge behind me.

'Goodbye, Bella!' I shouted. 'I've left a note for Sebastian. It's in the lounge. You might tell him when he comes in.'

When I got halfway back to the house, I stopped suddenly. Had I done the right thing? If Veronica had wanted Sebastian to read her letter, wouldn't she have written to him herself?

I stood still in the middle of the drive in an agony of indecision. Then I turned in my tracks and flew back to the cottage. I rushed round to the lounge window, which I knew was slightly open. If the note was still there, I could just reach it from outside, and Sebastian would never know. Anxiously I peeped into the room through one of the small, leaded window-panes. The room was still empty, but the note was gone!

My hair didn't take nearly as long to wash and trim as Fiona's did to 'set'. I filled in the time by reading *Punch* and watching through a crack in the curtain of the cubicle next to me a large lady with an incredibly thick neck having her hair cut in a 'Bubbles' style – that is to say, with curls all over her head, like a Greek statue.

'I like something *young*,' she was saying to the assistant. 'It's so important, nowadays, to look *young*, don't you think?'

The assistant murmured something polite, and I couldn't help thinking how much younger the large lady would have looked with a rather older hairstyle.

Fiona was being difficult over her 'set'. Several times she made the girl take out all the pins and combs and do it a different way, and even then she wasn't satisfied.

'I think it looks *frightful*,' she announced, when at length she emerged from underneath the drier. 'But I suppose it will just have to do. I expect everyone will think I've had a home perm or something awful. Can't you curl it a bit more round the sides?'

'That was the way I had it at first, miss,' countered the assistant. 'But you made me comb it out. I'm afraid it's too late now; it's dry, you see. I did say it would look rather bare—'

'I didn't mean you to leave *no* curls in at all,' snapped Fiona. 'I did think you'd use a little common-sense. Really the hairdresser who comes to our school does it better than this.'

'Then perhaps you'd better have it done at school in future, Miss Scott,' said the assistant, who by this time was looking very pink and annoyed, 'if we don't do it to your liking here.'

'Oh, don't be stupid!' exclaimed Fiona, putting her arms into the coat held out for her. 'I was only joking. Surely you can take a joke. Are you there, Caroline? Where's Trixie? I want her to pay the bill.'

'She's gone to the chemist's,' I said, 'and she paid the bill before she went. She said we had to go back to the car and wait for her when we were finished here. Thank you very much,' I added to the girl who had washed my hair. 'I hope you have a very happy New Year!'

'Thank you, Miss Caroline!' laughed the girl. 'Mind you don't go letting any young man first-foot you who hasn't got dark eyes!'

'I won't!' I promised.

As we left the hairdresser's I caught sight of Fiona and myself reflected in the long mirror near the door. It was very depressing. Fiona so tall and elegant, with her immaculately waved golden hair and blue eyes. Me, bucksome and rosy-cheeked, with dark brown eyes and my hair in a fringe, ending in two fat, black plaits. I had decided some time ago to let my hair grow long, but it certainly seemed to be taking its time about it!

It was late when we got back home, and after we'd had lunch and tea combined, there wasn't much time to go out riding before it got dark, so I slipped away, determined to find out if my efforts at making the peace between Sebastian and Veronica had been successful.

It was half past four, and the moon was already sailing over the tree-tops when I approached Sebastian's cottage for the third time that day. As before, there were no signs of Sebastian himself, and Bella seemed to have gone home. There were no lights in the lounge, so evidently Uncle Adrian hadn't got back from Newcastle yet. A glowing log fire lit up the room, and when I looked through the window, I could see signs that Sebastian had had a hasty meal, and then dashed out in the middle. There was a half-finished cup of tea on the top of the piano, and most of the toast Bella always provided was still sitting in its silver dish on the tea-trolley.

I opened the window farther, and let myself into the room, just in case Bella hadn't gone home. When one meets Bella, one just has to stay for a 'crack', as she calls it, and it was Sebastian I wanted to talk to just now.

For a long time I waited beside the fire, hoping he would return, but he didn't. I'm afraid I finished off the toast, and after that, two pieces of Bella's chocolate cake as well! Finally, I grew tired of waiting, so I swung myself over the window-sill again, closed the casement carefully behind me, and set off to look for him.

I searched for quite a long time without success. He wasn't in the little paddock exercising Warrior, his pony; nor was he down by the greenhouses talking to Daniel, the odd-job man; nor was he in the garage. I had almost given up the search when I suddenly thought of the lake, and set off towards it.

I had reached the little path leading to the tiny bathing beach before I saw him. He was sitting on the rough bench that runs along one side of the boathouse, and there was something about him that made me stop short suddenly before I'd made my presence known to him. He was leaning against the ramshackle wooden building, his head upon his arm, and in the hand nearest to me was something white. It might be – in fact, I knew it was – a letter. Veronica's letter!

Always before, when I had caught sight of Sebastian, I had yelled: 'Co-ee!' But now I stood silently on the snowy path, knowing that for some reason Sebastian was intensely miserable; that he'd come here to be alone; that he didn't want me or anyone else to see him in his misery. This was the strange thing about boys, I reflected. They hated to share their feelings. Girls were different. If I had been desperately unhappy, I'd probably have dissolved into tears on Trixie's ample shoulder, and told her all my troubles. But Sebastian, being a boy, preferred to fight his battles by himself.

I wondered what had been in Veronica's letter to upset him, but I couldn't think of anything. It had merely been a chatty letter, telling me all the news about rehearsals, and the people in the ballet, and surely the end part – the bit about Sebastian – had been kindness itself. But then, I reflected, Sebastian was a very strange boy. Things might upset him that wouldn't upset other people. Moreover, he was almost seventeen – nearly grown up, and when one is nearly grown up, things aren't quite so easy, or so comfortable. I heaved a sigh of relief. Thank goodness, I was only twelve! I shouldn't be grown up for years and years. Having come to this decision, I retraced my steps and went back to the Hall. Although I still didn't know whether my mission had been successful or not, I knew it was useless to beard the lion in his den – namely, Sebastian in his present mood!

Chapter 3

Angelo

THE next morning the sky was still cloudless. There was a hot sun and no wind, but the air was still so cold that although the snow melted on roofs and gables, you knew it wasn't a real thaw or 'fresh' as they call it here in Northumberland.

After breakfast I left Fiona trying on her frock for the Frazer's party, and hurried down the drive towards the gates where I could watch for the bus which, so Sebastian had told me, would bring Angelo from town. I perched myself on the wall overlooking the road, clearing away a patch of thick snow to do so. From Sebastian's cottage came the thundering chords of Beethoven's *Sonata Pathétique*. Sebastian had evidently got over his mood, and had forsaken the funeral marches for something mildly sad!

It wasn't long before the bus arrived, speeding with unaccustomed silentness along the snowy road. It stopped opposite the lodge gates and a boy got out. The *Sonata Pathétique* still filled the air, so I knew that Sebastian hadn't heard the bus stop. As for me, I took the opportunity of having a good look at the newcomer while I had the chance. He was slim and of medium height. At a distance I thought he wasn't unlike Sebastian himself, but as he came nearer I saw that he was a great deal darker. His skin was almost swarthy, and his eyes were so dark as to be almost black. They were wonderful eyes, melting one moment, flashing the next. His nose was highly bridged with thin, sensitive nostrils. His mouth was thin, too, and arrogantly curved.

I left my position of vantage on the wall and went forward to meet him.

'Oh, hullo! I expect you're Angelo? Sebastian told me about you.'

He turned, saw me, and gave me a funny little bow.

'Pleasure! I am *so* pleased to make your acquaintance. Yes, I am Angelo Ibañez. And you?'

'Oh, I'm Caroline,' I answered. 'Caroline Scott. I'm Sebastian's cousin. I live in the house up there among the trees' – I nodded towards the Hall – 'and Sebastian lives – but I expect you know all about Sebastian.'

Angelo smiled, showing a flash of strong, white teeth.

'Yes, I know quite a lot about Sebastian, as you say,' he admitted. 'But mostly about his music, not where he lives. You say?—' He motioned towards Uncle Adrian's pretty cottage with its overhanging eaves and blue door.

'He's expecting you,' I explained, 'but he began playing the *Sonata Pathétique*, and when Sebastian plays – well, you know how it is! He forgets everything else!'

'That I know also,' said Angelo with a shrug. His English, as Sebastian had said, was very good, but just a little stilted. 'We will arouse him – *so*!' Before I could go up to the door and bang on it, or shout 'Co-ee!' as I generally did, the newcomer put his hands into his jacket pocket, pulled out two brown objects, like conch-shells, fitted them over his thumbs, and beat a tattoo.

The *Pathétique* stopped as abruptly as if it had been switched off at the main.

'Angelo, old chap!' Sebastian appeared at the window. 'Don't say I never heard the bus!'

'You never hear anything when you are playing!' laughed Angelo. 'As your cousin, Caroline, says.'

'Oh, so you've met Caroline?' said Sebastian. 'Good! Saves me having to make introductions! Aren't you coming in?'

'What – this way?' Angelo stared at the window. 'You mean I am to climb through your window?'

I couldn't help laughing at his astonished face.

'Sebastian always asks you to climb in the window,' I said. 'He thinks it's original.'

'Well, isn't it?' countered Sebastian. 'Not many people ask you to climb in through their windows, do they? Come on, you two! Don't stand out there freezing!'

We climbed in, Angelo politely helping me up first, and Sebastian hauling me in not nearly so politely on the other side. To my relief, he seemed completely his old self again. I wondered whether he would refer to my note, or whether he would choose to ignore it. As if he read my thoughts, he dug his hand into his pocket, brought out an envelope, and handed it to me. I could see that he'd tried to smooth it out, but it was still very crumpled, and I knew instantly that I hadn't been mistaken – that it had been Veronica's letter he had held in his clenched hand yesterday.

'This belongs to you, Caroline,' he said quietly.

'Oh, then you found it all right,' I said unnecessarily, since, if he hadn't found it, he couldn't be holding it out now. 'Did you – did you read it, Sebastian?'

His mouth twisted.

'Yes – I read it.'

'Then you do understand?' I said eagerly. 'You will be friends with Veronica again?'

Sebastian sat down at the piano and ran his hands over the keys in a jangle of chords. Then he stopped playing and looked at me.

'No, I shall never be friends with Veronica again,' he said simply. After which he began to play *Claire de Lune* very quietly and sadly, and I knew that his mind was made up, and that it was no use arguing with him – not now, anyway. I think that Angelo felt the sense of strain in the air, for he said quickly:

'About this lake of yours, Sebastian? You did promise me some skating, you know.'

Sebastian stopped playing and got up from the piano stool.

'So I did, old chap. Well, it's just the day for it. Ice hard as nails. Leave your traps there' – he motioned to the lobby. 'We can see to them afterwards. Angelo's staying the night,' he added to me. 'He's going to the Frazers' party – mostly to support me, I may say. He knows how dearly I love the Frazers! Got your skates, Caroline?'

'Oh, yes,' I answered. 'I brought them along. Talk about virtuous! I actually remembered to grease them before I put them away last year.'

We walked down to the lake and put on our skates. Angelo proved to be an adept, and I stood on the edge of the ice watching his wonderful figure-eights and spins with wordless admiration.

'Wherever did you learn to skate like that?' I asked him when at last he glided over to me. 'Surely not in Spain?'

He laughed.

'No, not in Spain, as you say! I have learnt in Switzerland. Last winter I spend at Chamonix, paying for myself by dancing in the nights at the hotels there. *Ça va bien!*' He made a funny little gesture with his hands.

'It's no use talking French or any other language to Caroline!' laughed Sebastian. 'She's a hundred-per-cent English, and doesn't see the necessity of learning foreign languages.'

'No, of course not,' I countered. 'Why should I? As Mummy says, why bother trying to speak French when French people speak English so well?'

'A typical Aunt June statement!' declared Sebastian, who, I'm afraid, didn't like Mummy any more than she liked him. 'Golly! Look who's coming!'

We all turned round, and there was Fiona, dressed in her best brown velvet coat with a little hat to match, trimmed with dark fur. She was swinging a pair of skates in one hand, and incidentally they were very rusty.

'Oh, hullo, Fiona! I'd have waited for you, but you said you didn't want to come out because of your nose—' I began, but Fiona cut me short.

'I saw you all out of the bathroom window,' she explained,

giving Angelo a dazzling smile. 'And suddenly I thought I'd rather like to skate.'

She stood there waiting, so there was nothing for Sebastian to do but make the introductions.

'Oh, Fiona, this is Angelo Ibañez. Angelo, my cousin, Fiona Scott.'

Angelo bowed, though how he managed to do it on skates, and gracefully at that, I can't imagine!

Fiona smiled again, and then sat down on a log at the edge of the lake.

'If you're waiting for me to put your skates on for you, you've got the wrong idea!' Sebastian said with the lift of an eyebrow. 'Cousins never put on other cousins' skates for them, do they, Angelo, old chap?'

I think poor Angelo didn't quite know what to say, because Sebastian had not so very long ago put *my* skates on for me, and had evidently forgotten that fact in his usual way of forgetting things he didn't want to remember.

'If you will allow me,' the Spanish boy said politely. He knelt down on the ice, and deftly fixed Fiona's skates for her, whilst Sebastian looked on in silence. After a minute or two, he sat down himself and pointedly removed his own skates, as much as to say: 'This lake can hold either you or me, Fiona, but not both of us!'

'You lot can get on with your figure-eights,' he said, dropping his skates on the ice with a clatter. 'I'm off to collect wood for my fire.'

'W – what?' I stammered, horrified. 'Did you say a *fire*, Sebastian?'

'Yes, fire – F-I-R-E. Funny what a difficulty some people have with the English language. Oh, I didn't mean a fire in the middle of the lake. I shall make it over here on the beach. But you needn't be so scoffing about it, Caroline. Fires *have* been made on the ice, you know. One was made in the middle of the River Wear in eighteen-something, and kept alight for days and nights. And all the people came out of their houses and boiled the water for their afternoon cups of tea on it. Some of the worthy citizens even drove a fleet of buses across the ice – it was so hard.'

'I don't believe it,' declared Fiona. 'You're having us on.'

'What? Me tell you a tarradiddle?' said Sebastian solemnly. 'Never, dear lady!'

'Well, it wasn't what you said,' persisted Fiona. 'I've heard Daddy talk about that frightfully hard winter when the River Wear was frozen, and it was only for one night the fire was burning. It was a horse and cart that was driven across, not fleets of buses. I don't believe they had buses in those days, and you made up all that about the boiling water.'

'I assure you,' said Sebastian without a smile, 'it was as I say. I remember that nice, hot cup of tea distinctly. It was such a comfort on that cold February evening. Or was it January?'

'I thought you said it was in eighteen-something?' Fiona remarked sweetly.

'Oh, did I? I must have meant nineteen. These centuries are so confusing. I can never get them right! Of course, I remember now, it was last winter. How careless of me!'

'Last winter was very mild,' said Fiona. 'We didn't have a single hard frost last winter.'

'Oh, didn't we? Then, I must have been thinking of some other chap,' Sebastian said, nothing daunted. 'The chap who drank the tea, I mean. Excuse me, Fiona! I want that log you're sitting on for my fire. I'll just shake off the surplus woodlice, shall I? I always think roast sausages are so much more tasty then roast creepie-crawlies.'

Fiona got up so quickly that she slipped on the ice and fell down with a crash.

'You *are* beastly!' she exclaimed as Angelo and I helped her up. 'I don't believe one word you say! I don't believe there *are* any woodlice. Anyway, if there are, they'll all be frozen and dead long ago.'

'Dear me, no,' said Sebastian. 'Where is your natural history, Fiona? Woodlice don't die in the winter: they hibernate, and come to life as perky as perky on warm days! I shouldn't wonder if a good few haven't come to life with you sitting on that log. They certainly will when I get my fire going. They'll think it's midsummer! I do hope some haven't dropped down inside your boots, Fiona, all rolled up in balls.'

Fiona gave a hasty glance down at her fur-lined boots. Then I think she realized that Sebastian was only baiting her, so she turned her back on him.

'Oh, come on, let's skate!' she cried impatiently.

To be strictly fair, Fiona skated rather well – much better than me. Angelo spent his time teaching us in turns. By lunchtime I had managed the 'outside edge', and Fiona had done a rather wild figure-eight.

'What a pity Veronica isn't here,' I said regretfully, as we sat down to rest on an upturned boat. 'She'd have been wonderful at skating. So graceful! I can just imagine Veronica doing *Les Patineurs* on this lake.'

Sebastian was over on the far side of the little beach, but I saw him stiffen at the sound of Veronica's name. He came over and stood looking down at us with the funniest expression on his face.

'You seem to forget that skating is rather different from ballet – especially skating out of doors,' he declared. 'Personally, I think ballet is overrated. I used to be keen on it once, but now I think it's artificial and stupid.'

I said nothing, because I knew perfectly well that Sebastian wasn't speaking the truth. He loved ballet as much as ever, but he was still angry with poor Veronica because she had dared to put her ballet before his concert. Angelo, however, was completely taken in. He nodded eagerly.

'Yes, that is what I think. Ballet is so artificial, is it not? Now dancing in Spain – ah, that is all fire and vitality!'

'Go on – let's have a demonstration!' urged Sebastian.

But Angelo only shook his head and laughed.

'Oh, no! Not on the ice. I think that ice and the Spanish dance do not mix together. Ice-cream and fire! No, no, no!'

'Oh, well, if you won't, you won't,' said Sebastian. 'Then, if we can't have some Spanish dancing, how about some sausages?'

'Oh, rather!' I said. 'But have you got any?'

Sebastian pretended to search in all his pockets.

'Dear, dear! I could swear I had a sausage somewhere. But never mind, I can easily achieve a few,' he declared. 'I have a notion that dear Bella was going to provide a sausage lunch, How about my toddling back home and breaking the glad news to her that we'll be lunching down here. We could have the sausages as first course, and ice-cream – freshly dug from the lake – for a sweet.'

'Good idea!' we said in chorus.

'I'll go back home, too,' I offered, 'and beg something from Trixie to swell the feast. It's too bad for you to have to provide everything, Sebastian. How about you, Fiona? You could help to carry the loot!'

But Fiona said she'd stay down by the lake with Angelo and keep the fire going, so Sebastian and I went off on our separate errands.

Sebastian got back first. He managed to get eight sausages, a loaf of newly-baked bread, a piece of butter wrapped up in greaseproof paper, and his pockets were filled with biscuits, quite a few chocolate ones amongst them. It was plain to be seen that Bella was Sebastian's slave, just as Trixie was!

I did rather well, too. I persuaded Trixie to part with half a loaf of gingerbread, four slices of fruit cake, and four oranges.

'All we need now is something to drink,' I said when I arrived back on the shores of the lake.

'Your wish is granted, lady,' said Sebastian promptly, digging his hand into his jacket pocket and fishing out a tin of cocoa.

'Yes, but—'

'Oh, you mean kettle, and so on—' He disappeared into the

boathouse and emerged a few minutes later with a battered and somewhat rusty kettle, and an ancient teapot with half its spout missing.

'Gracious!' I laughed. 'I'd forgotten those things! Now if we only had some milk—'

'Some people,' observed Sebastian, digging once more into his pocket and drawing out a small tin of condensed milk, 'are never satisfied. *Now* what more do you require? State your wishes, lady. Don't mind me!'

'Oh, there's *nothing* else,' I said. 'We've got simply *everything*.'

'Except cups,' said Fiona flatly.

We looked at each other.

'Well, we could always drink out of our shoes,' began Sebastian, taking one off and looking at it speculatively. 'But perhaps Fiona wouldn't like—'

'I should just think not!' exclaimed Fiona with a shudder. 'What a positively *revolting* idea!'

'Oh, I assure you it was often done in the best theatrical and ballet circles,' Sebastian told her. 'They always drank their champagne out of Pavlova's ballet shoe. I believe they ate the shoe afterwards as hors-d'oeuvre. But, of course, if you don't like the idea ... *Honi soi qui mal de mer,* as Shakespeare said, or was it Milton? Evil be to him that evil thinks.'

'You've got it all wrong,' said Fiona. 'I learnt that in our French idiom lesson at school, and *mal de mer* means seasick.'

'Oh, well, seasickness is an evil, isn't it?'

'Yes, but—'

'Don't let's argue. Let's think about the problem on hand – cups, or rather the lack of them.'

'I know!' I shrieked. 'We can put the cocoa in someone's hankie, and drink out of the cocoa tin in turns.'

'Brainwave, as usual, Caroline!' declared Sebastian.

'Yes – as long as it isn't *my* hankie,' said Fiona firmly.

After we had solved the problem of the cups, our picnic went off smoothly. I was amazed at Fiona. She quite seemed to like having lunch out in the snow. She had evidently forgotten all about her nose, and she didn't mention chilblains once.

We stayed down by the frozen lake until the moon rose over the snowy tree-tops, and Sebastian's watch said three o'clock. Finally, Fiona said that she thought she ought to go home. For one thing, Trixie would be expecting us back for tea, and for another – this I guessed was the real reason – we ought to be getting ready for the party.

'But it isn't until six o'clock!' I exclaimed. 'You don't want two whole hours to get ready for the Frazers' party!'

'Yes, I do,' declared Fiona. 'I want to have a bath—'

'But you had a bath last night,' I argued.

Fiona grew pink.

'I wish you'd stop discussing my washing arrangements!' she snapped.

'I didn't! It was you who—'

'Oh, shut up!'

We gave in for peace's sake, and packed up the picnic things regretfully. We left the boys where the path divided, and Fiona and I went on up to the Hall.

'Got a surprise for you tonight!' Sebastian called after us, his voice thin and clear in the frosty air.

'Now I wonder what it can be?' I said curiously.

'Oh, nothing really exciting, I expect,' Fiona answered, tossing her head. 'I expect it'll be something terribly stupid. He'll turn up in a white tie and tails, or come dressed in sheets of music, or something!'

Chapter 4

Mostly about a Party

As a matter of fact, Sebastian's surprise really *was* a surprise this time! He and Angelo arrived at the front door of Bracken Hall with a real sleigh, drawn by Warrior, Sebastian's pony. Even Fiona couldn't help giving a gasp of admiration when she saw the neat little turnout.

'Oh, Sebastian! What a perfectly wonderful idea!' I exclaimed. 'Will he pull it, do you think?'

'Who? Warrior? I should think so,' answered Sebastian offhandedly. 'I tried him out yesterday, and he went OK. If he won't pull it, then we shall just have to pull *him*!'

'You – you mean we're going over to the Frazers in it?' Fiona said doubtfully, looking down at her high-heeled party shoes.

'That's the general idea,' said Sebastian. 'I think it would be wiser if you included some bootees, or galoshes, or something amongst your ever-so-elegant equipment, dear Cousin Fiona – just in case we have to leg it!'

Fiona didn't know what to say. You could see she didn't want to take off her satin slippers and velvet party cloak, and substitute an old mac and Wellingtons, but on the other hand she certainly didn't want us to drive off in the sleigh without her, leaving her to follow, in solitary splendour, in the car with Perkins.

'Oh, all right,' she said at length. 'I expect it would be wiser!'

It was lovely driving along the snowy roads in the moonlight. Sebastian had fixed a couple of old carriage lamps, complete with candles, on either side of the sleigh, and there were bells jingling on the reins and on the collar of Warrior's harness. Fiona and I sat in state, covered with an old leopard-skin rug that Sebastian said he had pinched out of his bedroom. Angelo sat just behind us, and Sebastian drove the team – I mean Warrior – standing upright. He cracked his whip at intervals, and at each crack Warrior leapt forward like a kangaroo, and we were nearly shot out. Still, it was wonderful!

Angelo didn't say very much. There was a far-away look in his dark eyes, as if he were thinking of other things. Evidently Sebastian noticed this, for presently he stopped cracking his whip and said pointedly: 'A penny for them, old chap? Were you thinking of Spain, or perhaps of some fair – or should I say dark? – *señorita*?'

Angelo came back to earth with a start.

'You ask for my thoughts? They were far away in the streets of Seville. There it is hot all the year round – unlike this place where it is always cold. Yes, even in the middle of the summer!'

'Oh, no, Angelo – not in the summer!'

'Northumberland is never more than – how do you say it? – lukewarm, even in a heat wave,' insisted Angelo. 'Although it is beautiful, too; that I admit.'

'Never mind. Do go on, Angelo. You were going to tell us about Spain.'

'Perhaps some of my thoughts were in Granada,' went on Angelo, 'among the gipsies.'

Sebastian cracked his whip again, and began to hum Ravel's *Bolero*. Angelo took out his castanets and began to play them, and poor Warrior thought his end had come, and leapt forward as if he were shot!

It wasn't very far to Lingfield, where the Frazers lived, and in less than an hour we saw below us a clump of dark fir trees that told us we were nearing our journey's end.

'Lingfield Lodge,' Sebastian said, pointing with his whip. 'Our blissful destination – I *don't* think! I'm referring to the blissful! Say, you lot, wouldn't it be a joke if we lured all the unhappy guests away from the Lodge – like the Pied Piper lured the rats – and took 'em off sledging, instead of letting 'em stew in the Frazer's awful drawing-room?'

'Oh, Sebastian, we couldn't!' I said, horrified. 'Poor Mrs Frazer will have got everything prepared. It would be most unkind.'

'Of course we couldn't,' snapped Fiona. I think that by now the novelty of the sleigh had worn off, and her feet were cold, so she was in a bad temper. 'Sebastian was only joking of course.'

But I, for one, wasn't too sure! Looking at Sebastian, as he stood silhouetted darkly against the pale sky like an avenging angel, I felt that he might easily do as he threatened. He had no ideas of right and proper behaviour, had Sebastian, when he was dealing with people he didn't like! I couldn't help feeling a little uneasy, and wishing that Mummy hadn't insisted upon our coming. But, as it happened, my fears proved to be groundless this time. Sebastian behaved very well, all things considered.

'Gosh! Look at all the lights!' he exclaimed as we reached the wrought-iron gates at the bottom of the drive. 'What a waste of electricity!'

'Oh, well – they generate their own,' said Fiona, 'so it's their own affair.'

'That doesn't say they ought to *waste* it,' argued Sebastian. 'People oughtn't to waste things – even if they *are* disgustingly rich. You wouldn't go driving your car over the rough moor and breaking all its springs just because you could get another one by whistling for it, would you?'

Sebastian was really trying to vex Fiona, because this is just the sort of thing she did. She'd run about in the heather in her best stockings and shoes, and then, when Trixie told her off about it, she'd say loftily: 'Mummy will get me some more the first time we're in town.' I'm afraid that Fiona was dreadfully spoilt. Even though I was her sister, I couldn't help realizing it.

The Frazers' house really looked very nice when we piled out of the sleigh and trooped into the big, square hall. Sebastian had taken the sleigh and Warrior round to the stables.

Lingfield Lodge wasn't an old house like Bracken Hall, but it was warm and comfortable, and everything that money could buy had evidently been bought. As Sebastian had said, the Frazers were digustingly rich. The Lodge had originally been a couple of farm cottages and a few broken-down outbuildings. The Frazers had knocked the two cottages into one, added a wing to the south-east, which they had made into a beautiful lounge with wide plate-glass windows all round one end, so that you could watch the cloud shadows over the hillsides opposite and imagine you were outside. There was a paved terrace, too, where you could sit whenever it was warm enough and listen to the splash of a waterfall as it hurled itself over a stony crag on the moors above. An upper storey had been added, as well, giving the Lodge several more bedrooms, and the dilapidated outbuildings had been repaired and made into a garage and stables. The whole thing was built round a little paved courtyard with a statue in the middle, and the effect was lovely, even though it *was* modern. In fact, the only drawback about it was the Frazers themselves! None of us liked them. Ian, like Fiona, was almost grown up, so it didn't matter so much about him, but Maud was awful, too. She always wanted to win everything, and cried when she didn't. Also, she wasn't above cheating, which wasn't surprising because Ian cheated, too, so you couldn't really blame her for that. Added to this, she was always boasting about her parents' wealth. The first thing she said, when she saw our admiring glances cast upon the lovely Christmas tree blazing with electric lights, was:

'There's a present on it for each of you. Real presents, too, very expensive ones, not just crackers and things. Oh, and thank you all for the Christmas card. Ruth Fisher sent me one exactly the same last year, only hers was a calendar.'

'Then how could it be exactly the same?' demanded Sebastian, who had just come in from the stables and had heard her remark.

'Oh, well, you know what I mean. The *picture* on it was the same,' persisted Maud. 'Only, of course, hers was bigger.'

'Bigger, better, and brighter!' murmured Sebastian sarcastically. 'It *would* be!'

We played games till supper-time. They were the sort of games where you have to work things out on paper and *think* all the time – not exciting games like Murder and Blind Man's Buff.

'I shall be either grey or bald by the end of this evening's so-called entertainment,' declared Sebastian. 'So much bally thinking gets a man down!'

'Hush! Maud is just over there. She'll hear you,' I cautioned him.

'Don't care if she does,' said Sebastian naughtily. 'People who make you *think* at a party ought to be drowned at birth!'

Fortunately, before Sebastian's ebony locks had turned grey, supper-time arrived and saved the situation. We all sat down at two big tables in the dining-room, and the six grown-ups stood about with cups of coffee in their hands and waited upon us. We knew most of the other guests. In fact, there were only two completely strange ones – a girl called Jane Foster, and her cousin, Nigel Monkhouse. We gathered that Jane lived at a country house called Monks Hollow, about six miles away, and Nigel at Bychester Tower, two miles nearer Lingfield. Nigel's father was Sir Robert Monkhouse, squire of the village of Bychester. Nigel was big and fair, and he bossed poor little Jane about like anything. Jane was very small and pale, and she looked years younger than Nigel, although, as a matter of fact, we found out that there was only a year between them, Nigel being eleven and Jane ten.

'And how did you manage to get over here, dear?' asked Mrs Frazer of Jane. 'We quite expected a telephone call saying the road was still blocked by snow.'

'Yes, it is,' Jane said. 'But Mummy rode over with me as far as the bottom of your drive—'

'Yes, and Jane's to go back with me after the party,' Nigel broke in. 'She's staying at our place for the night. Aren't you, Jane? Your mother said you had to.'

'Y-es,' Jane said, not very happily, it seemed to me.

There were five other people at our table. A very tall, dark boy, called Guy Charlton, whom we knew slightly. He'd ridden over from Hordon Castle, about seven miles away. Next to him was his cousin, David Eliot, who lived at Dewburn Hall. He'd come over by car, and his small sister, Patience, should have come with him, but she'd got a cold and had had to stay at home in bed. After this came the Moffits – John and Lillian. Their father was the vicar of Bychester. At the end of the table was Ian Frazer. He sat next to Fiona, and talked to her all the time, which wasn't very polite of him, but I don't expect anybody minded.

Mrs Frazer, in the intervals of passing sandwiches, and taking away cups to be refilled, was explaining to a tall, dark lady, who, it seemed from the conversation, lived in London, the difficulties of having a children's party in the wilds of Northumberland.

'If you have it during the Christmas holidays, you're nearly sure to be snowed up, and half the children can't come,' she said. 'So different to when we lived in Blackpool.'

'I expect it was!' answered the dark lady with a smile. 'But you seem to have done very well, notwithstanding.'

'Yes, it amazes me the way they've managed to get here,' went on Mrs Frazer. 'On horseback, quite a lot of them. I must say they're not lacking in ingenuity. I was tickled to death with the Scotts. They came in a sleigh, complete with jingle-bells!' She laughed, and, as Sebastian said, she did sound a bit like a hyena! I could see him bristle. Sebastian didn't like to be laughed at – not by Mrs Frazer, anyway!

All through supper I kept thinking of the vow I'd made to Trixie at the breakfast table yesterday, and somehow I managed not to have two helpings of anything – even ice-cream. It took a tremendous amount of will-power, I can tell you!

After supper, the party brightened up a bit. For one thing, David Eliot's sister, Patience, caused a sensation by arriving at the party after all. She'd walked across the moor from Dewburn with only her slippers on! We all had to rush round getting dry clothes and hot drinks for her. Fortunately, Maud's clothes were about the same size. Then, after we'd got Patience settled, someone suggested Musical Chairs for the younger ones, and Charades for the others. After this we played a game called Old Mrs McGinty's Dead. You had to say: 'Old Mrs McGinty died shaking her head like *this*.' The person speaking had to shake his or her head, after which the next person had to copy it, and add something else, such as: 'Old Mrs McGinty's dead. She died shaking her head like *this*, and waggling her arm like *that*!' And so on. If you didn't get the rigmarole right, you had to pay a forfeit. After it had been round the room a couple of times, it got so complicated that nearly everyone got it wrong, so at the end of the game there was a huge pile of forfeits – hairslides, slippers, hankies, watches, bracelets, and all sorts of wearing apparel.

Ian volunteered to kneel down and tell the person the forfeit belonged to what they had to do to get it back again. Fiona helped him.

'Here's a thing and a very pretty thing,' chanted Fiona, holding up a white hankie over Ian's head. 'What has the owner of this pretty thing to do?'

'Kiss four bare legs!' ordered Ian.

It was mine, and I knew what to do. I dashed over to a chair, and kissed each leg in turn.

The next forfeit was a hairslide, and it belonged to Maud.

'Put yourself up the chimney!' ordered Ian.

Poor Maud stood first on one leg, then on the other.

'Go on, stupid!' exclaimed Ian, looking up from his lowly position at Fiona's feet. 'Write "Yourself" on a bit of paper and put it up the chimney.'

The last forfeit to be read out was Angelo's. It was one of his cuff-links.

'Dance in the middle of the room!' commanded Ian, just as if he knew who the forfeit belonged to, though he swore afterwards he didn't.

Angelo stood for a moment, hesitating, and while he stood there, Sebastian stole into the alcove where the piano stood in darkness. The next moment the Frazers' lounge was filled with the compelling rhythm of a Flamenco gipsy dance. Angelo still remained perfectly still for a second or two. Then he drew himself up, hands above his head, fingers pointed. Then his castanets began to click.

I had never seen anything like Angelo's dancing, and neither, I'm sure, had the Frazers. All eyes were fixed upon that slender figure in the middle of the room, his stamping feet beating out the intricate rhythm, his strong fingers positively making the castanets talk. The huge burst of clapping at the end of his performance showed how thrilled we were with his dancing. We knew, instinctively, that what we had seen was no mere drawing-room performance. We had been watching a talented *artiste*. One and all we crowded round him, and the dark-haired lady grew quite excited.

'Oh, do show us how to do it!' we all shouted in chorus. 'Teach one of us, please! Which one shall it be? Choose!'

'Choose *me*!' begged Fiona. 'I've learnt dancing longer than any of them. Choose *me*!'

'No! No! No!' laughed Angelo. 'I am sorry, Fiona, but to me you do not look like a Spanish dancer. Nor you! Nor you! There is only one person here—' He glanced rapidly at the group of girls clustered round him. 'Only one who looks like a Spanish gipsy. That is you, Caroline.'

'Me?' I said in surprise.

'Yes, you, Caroline. Come! Do this!' He showed me a step. 'Toss the head, so! Swing the skirt! Oh, never mind if you have not a long one to swing. Make the pretence! Swing the hips, so!'

I did as he commanded, and Angelo's face grew radiant.

'But, Caroline, you are a *trained* dancer! I did not know!'

'A ballet dancer,' I corrected him. 'At least, I've had ballet lessons, but I'm not very good.'

'Oh, but you are *wonderful*! Wonderful!' he declared. 'I could make of you a Spanish dancer in no time at all! You are the right build; you have the right figure and face – dark, like a Flamenco. You have the warmth and the fire. Why did I not think of it before? It is a thousand pities I go away to the south almost immediately. But never mind – next year I return, and then we shall see!'

Next year? I said nothing. It seemed foolish to tell him that by next year, if my wild plan succeeded – the plan I'd been turning over in my mind ever since Veronica had gone back to London – I shouldn't be here.

'We shall see!' I laughed. 'And thank you for the lesson!'

'What about Sebastian?' someone said. '*He* hasn't redeemed his forfeit.'

'He didn't have to give anything,' came Sebastian's voice from the alcove. 'Trust Sebastian! He always was a wily old serpent!'

'Oh, never mind – play us something, Sebastian,' said the quiet, dark lady. 'I've heard how well you play.'

Sebastian was never loath to oblige in that direction. He began to play, very softly, one of Chopin's waltzes – the Waltz from *Les Sylphides*.

I'm afraid people weren't listening to him as they ought to have done – people don't at a party – but I don't think Sebastian minded. I felt he wasn't playing to us, really, but to the ghost of Veronica – Veronica in a washed-out cotton frock and bare feet, with her dark hair tossed back and her face lifted towards the shadow of a new moon, caught in the branches of the fir trees, Veronica dancing on the dewy grass outside his window like the spirit of Spring itself. In that haunting melody Sebastian poured out all his unhappiness and disappointment.

I was so busy listening to Sebastian that I just heard the tail end of an excited conversation between Angelo and the dark-haired lady. Her name, it appeared, was Delgardo, and, like Angelo, she was of Spanish extraction. It seemed she was one of the dance producers of television programmes.

'And if ever you want to appear on television, just apply to me, and I'll arrange an audition for you,' she said, seriously, to Angelo. 'Of course, after the audition you would have a camera test, but I think you would do very well.' She glanced with a practised eye at the boy's clear-cut features and animated expression. 'Yes, I am sure of it.'

'I'll remember,' promised Angelo. 'But first I must have a partner. How about you, Caroline?'

'What, you mean seriously?'

'Naturally.'

'Oh, no,' I said. 'I don't think I could. I mean, I don't think I want to. Besides—'

'Besides what?' he persisted.

'Oh, nothing,' I laughed. 'Only I think you'd better get someone else. I'm not old enough, for one thing.'

'That is true,' Angelo said with a little bow. 'But only for the moment. I forget that I am several years older than you are. But never mind – for the time being I will find another partner and content myself with her, but some day – some day, I shall dance with you, Caroline. I feel it in the gipsy part of me that tells me of the future.'

If Angelo had been an English boy, I expect we'd have laughed at him, but as it was nobody as much as smiled.

'We shall see,' I said.

Chapter 5

Guy Takes a Hand

BEFORE we went home, Mr Frazer, dressed as Santa Claus, gave us all presents off the Christmas tree. Mine was a tail-bandage for Gillyflower, my pony, and Sebastian's was a gramophone record. It was some of the dances in the ballet suite *Carnival*, and it was Myra Hess playing them. Sebastian was frightfully pleased with his present – in fact, I think he almost forgave the Frazers for asking him to their party! He went off with Ian to put it on the radiogram straight away.

While the rest of us received our presents, we could hear the plaintive Pierrot melody saying: 'Oh, de-ear me!' from the distant lounge where the radiogram was.

Fiona had a very beautiful present. It was a brooch made in the form of a basket of flowers – the flowers being different-coloured stones. I have an idea that Ian had arranged a specially expensive gift in order to impress her. If so, he was certainly successful. Fiona smiled like a Cheshire cat, and said goodbye to the Frazers in her most dazzling manner. I have to admit that Fiona can be pretty devastating when she chooses!

After all the presents had been given out we had cups of soup, and then it was time to go home. Guy Charlton rode with us part of the way, as Hordon is in our direction. I pretended our sleigh was an old-fashioned coach, and that Guy was an outrider to protect us from highwaymen and wolves!

We hadn't gone far when Sebastian said: 'Hullo! I wonder who that is?' He pointed with his whip towards the far corner of the field on our right. The stream ran through it, and in the bright moonlight we could see two figures on horseback standing on the bank.

'It's Nigel Monkhouse, and that Jane girl,' Fiona said. 'I forget her name.'

'You mean Jane Foster?' I put in. 'Yes, I think you're right. I wonder what they're doing down there? Perhaps it's a short cut to wherever it is they live.'

Then, in the cold, frosty air, their voices reached us.

'Come on!' Nigel said. 'It's no use dithering there, Jane. Don't be such a little coward. You've *got* to jump it. There isn't a bridge, and you know it.'

'I – I think I'll go round by the road – if you don't mind, Nigel,' came Jane's nervous treble.

We saw Nigel catch hold of her bridle to stop her.

'But I *do* mind! It's miles and miles that way. You don't catch me riding round there with you when there's a perfectly good short cut. Now, come along, Jane, and don't waste so much time. It's blessed cold standing here!'

'I – I'll fall in.'

'You won't if you do as I say and let Dapple have her head. If you pull her back, you'll jolly well deserve a wetting!'

'But it's so c-cold!' we heard Jane say miserably.

'You wouldn't be cold if you only *rode* your pony, and didn't just sit on her like a wet weekend!' declared Nigel.

It was at this moment that we heard a slight movement behind us. We had all been so fascinated by what was going on in the field that we'd quite forgotten Guy Charlton. He now leaned down from the back of his big, black pony, Flyaway, and quietly opened the gate into the meadow.

'Half a moment! Shan't be long!'

He rode up to the shivering Jane and said something to her, but we couldn't hear what it was. Then we saw her dismount. After which, we saw Guy bend down towards her and help her to mount behind him on Flyaway.

'Hold tight to me, kid!' we heard him yell. 'Round my waist! Hold on, now!'

The next moment Flyaway was over the stream with his double burden like a bird.

'Hi!' yelled Nigel. 'What do you think you're doing? What about her pony? I can't jump them both across, can I?'

'No, I'm afraid you'll have to lead them across,' stated Guy.

'In all that cold water! What do you take me for?'

'Nothing else for it, I'm afraid,' insisted Guy smoothly.

'How about you jumping back and leading one of them across for me?' suggested Nigel.

'That would leave Jane standing in the snow,' said Guy, and we could hear a certain note in his voice that told us, and Nigel too, that he would stand no nonsense. 'Better take your shoes off, old chap, and be quick about it.'

Seeing that there was nothing else for it, Nigel obeyed. He took off his shoes and socks, tied them round his neck, and waded into the icy stream, leading his pony, and his cousin's as well. Personally, I couldn't help admiring the cheerful way he accepted defeat. All he said was: 'Gosh! It's jolly cold!' Even when he stepped on a stone and went in up to the middle of his thighs, he didn't murmur. Although he was a terribly bossy boy and led poor Jane an awful life, you couldn't help seeing his good points.

'I hope there aren't any more streams between here and your home?' Guy said, as he helped Jane to mount again.

'Not one. Word of honour!' Nigel said with a grin. 'Perhaps I *was* a bit hard on the kid, but she's such a little sissy when it comes to horses. So long! Expect I shall see you again some time.'

They swung off through the woods, and all that remained to tell the tale were the imprints of their ponies' hooves on the snowy ground.

We drove on until we came to the crossroads which was where our ways parted.

'So long!' Guy yelled, swinging away to the left. 'Happy New Year!'

'Goodbye!' we shouted after him. 'A Happy New Year to you!'

'What a nice boy,' I said, half to myself. 'So big and strong, yet ever so gentle.'

'Bossy I thought him!' said Fiona. 'Personally, I didn't think there was much to choose between him and that awful little Nigel Monkhouse.'

'By the way,' put in Sebastian, 'Guy's just reminded me. It's nearly twelve o'clock and it's New Year's Eve – Hogmanay across the Border. In five minutes it'll be the beginning of the New Year. Let's see it in here, shall we?'

We sat in the sleigh on the top of a hilly piece of ground with the snowy countryside spread out before us like a white eiderdown. Here and there lights twinkled, telling us of the presence of remote farmsteads whose owners were also seeing the New Year in, North Country fashion.

There wasn't a sound except for that faint singing in the air I've described before. The dark-blue midnight sky blazed with stars, and the moon sailed amongst them like a great round shining cheese.

'No factory whistles here!' said Sebastian. 'No colliery hooters, fog-horns, or, in fact, anything – except *that*!' The weird cry of a screech-owl, seeking its prey, shattered the absolute silence.

'And that!' I added, as a fox howled from a nearby covert. 'You think it's silent in the country, yet it isn't really.'

'You can't call that *noise*,' said Sebastian. 'It's really all part of the silence. Well, it's twelve o'clock, folks – the witching hour! We'd better be getting on, or they'll be sending out search parties for us! Happy New Year, everyone! May all your dreams come true!'

We all stayed quite still for a moment, wishing. I expect Sebastian wished that he might become a famous conductor or concert pianist, Fiona that she would marry someone with an awful lot of money – Ian Frazer, for instance – Angelo that he might become a renowned Spanish dancer. As for me – I'm not telling anyone *my* wish, because everyone knows if you tell your wishes, they don't come true!

Summer

Chapter 1

Fiona and I Quarrel

One night at the end of February, just when we had come to regard the white world as ours for ever, a warm west wind came, and in the morning the snow had vanished from the fields like a dream. Of course, it was still piled up in blocks at the sides of the roads, but it was nice to see the green grass again. And how green it was! 'Living emerald!' as Sebastian put it poetically. The ponies kicked up their heels, and were exceedingly happy. When we turned them out, they straightway began to roll on the soft, squelchy ground as if they, too, knew it was spring!

Then the birds began to sing. First the robin, then the tiny sedge-warbler with his piercingly sweet bubbling notes, flung into the air like a handful of bells. Then came the lonely cry of the curlew, wheeling in endless flight over the moorland, and the plaintive mewing call of the peewit. Almost before we realized it, May had arrived, and with it the songless swallows, diving and swooping noiselessly round the eaves of the old house, in and out of the stables and other outbuildings. I couldn't help thinking how mysterious they were, coming back each year to their same old haunts for just these few summer months.

May passed, and the rhododendrons flowered in the woods round Bracken Hall. The bell-heather and gorse blazed on the moorland, the buttercups varnished the pastures round the house, the bracken uncurled its fronds, and waved as high as our heads. Summer came in with such a triumphant blaze of purple and gold that you could almost hear it!

Only one thing marred the happiness I felt at the passing of winter, and that was the absence of Sebastian. He'd gone to London on the 30th of April – Veronica's birthday – to study at the Royal College of Music, and since Fiona had gone back to her Harrogate school, I was all by myself. Fortunately, I was so busy at school and at my new ballet classes that I hadn't time to be lonely. I worked so hard at my ballet that, to my great joy, Miss Martin said I could take my first major RAD examination, the Elementary, at the end of the summer term. To my amazement, I got Honours! Miss Martin was nearly as thrilled as I was!

At the beginning of the holidays a friend of Mummy's, Lady Blantosh, who lives near us, came to tea. Usually I find her rather boring, but this time she gave me the thrill of my life by remarking: 'Why, Caroline! I hardly knew you, child! What have you been doing to yourself?'

'D-doing, Lady Blantosh? What do you mean?'

'You've gone so *thin*,' she grumbled. Lady Blantosh is on the stout side herself, so she doesn't like slim people. 'Surely your mother hasn't allowed you to diet?'

Mummy looked at me anxiously, and I said nothing, hoping to goodness Trixie wouldn't give me away.

'Oh, girls often slim down when they get to Caroline's age,' Mummy said. 'I remember Fiona was quite plump when she was thirteen. It's what I call puppy fat.'

When Lady Blantosh had gone – I thought of her as 'dear Lady Blantosh' now! – I dashed upstairs to the bathroom and stared at myself in the big mirror. Yes, it was true! You couldn't call me as slender as a willow-wand, but there was no doubt about it – I certainly wasn't *fat*. It was a wonderful moment! I felt like offering up a prayer of thanksgiving to all the second helpings of ice-cream I hadn't eaten! Fiona, who'd just come home from school was unimpressed, though.

'I don't know what you want to be slim for,' she said 'Anyone would think you were going to be a stupid ballet dancer, like Veronica.'

'Perhaps I am,' I said.

Fiona burst out laughing.

'I'd like to see *you* doing *Les Sylphides*,' she scoffed. 'A pretty substantial spirit *you'd* make – even if you are a bit slimmer than you used to be!'

Yes, Fiona wasn't a very agreeable companion, these days. I don't know what was the matter with her; I heard Florence, our cook, say to Trixie, when she thought I wasn't listening, that Miss Fiona seemed to be a bit disgruntled nowadays. 'It'll be because of the change in their fortunes, I shouldn't wonder,' she added. 'Them as has grown up with a silver spoon in their mouths – not to say golden – takes to it badly when the crash comes.'

'What crash?' I asked. 'What do you mean?'

'Never you mind, Miss Caroline,' Florence said. 'I didn't know you were there. Now don't you go telling the mistress what I said, there's a good child.'

'Of course not, if you don't want me to,' I said. All the same, I wondered what she meant.

Fiona always seemed to be wanting things. First it was riding lessons at school.

'But you don't need anyone to teach you how to ride,' Mummy expostulated. 'Why, you've had a pony all your life. You can ride at home if you really want to, and save all that expense. I'm sure it would do poor Melisande good to have a little more exercise.'

Fiona sighed.

'You don't understand, Mummy. I want to ride *at school* – not here. Everyone rides.'

'Oh, surely not *everyone*?' said Mummy.

'Everyone who is anyone,' said Fiona enigmatically. 'It's really frightful the way I can never do the things other people do, or have the things they have. Practically everyone has a portable wireless—'

'What, the whole school?' I said with a giggle. 'Gosh! What a noise there must be!'

'Don't be silly, Caroline!' snapped Fiona. 'Of course, I didn't mean that. Really, you are ridiculous. I meant practically everyone in the Sixth Form.'

'Well, I'm afraid you can't have a portable wireless just yet,' said Mummy flatly. 'Perhaps at Christmas—'

'It's always "perhaps at Christmas"!' cried Fiona in exasperation. 'And then when Christmas comes I get a mouldy twinset. Something useful!'

I saw the worried lines deepen on Mummy's face, and suddenly I noticed that her hair had turned quite grey. My wrath against my sister flared up.

'Fiona! You are beastly!' I yelled. 'If Mummy can't afford to give you expensive presents, she can't! And that twinset was real cashmere, and it was beautiful—'

'Oh, all right! All right!' said Fiona with a shrug. 'I was only *saying*.'

'I was wondering,' Mummy said, trying, I think, to change the subject, 'if you would like to ride into the village, Fiona, and give these tickets to Mrs Musgrave. They're for the Women's Institute concert on Friday. She gave me twelve to sell, and I'm afraid I only managed to get rid of six!'

'Oh, but we *can't* return half of them,' said Fiona. 'What on earth would Mrs Musgrave think? Why, we always buy the ones we can't sell ourselves—'

'I'm afraid we can't do that this year,' said Mummy with a sigh. 'You see, we really must economize, Fiona—'

'Economize! Economize!' shouted Fiona. 'I'm sick of the word! Anyway, I can't ride into the village in these jodhpurs. They're far too small, and if you won't get me some new ones—'

'I'll go! I'll go, Mummy!' I cried. 'Oh, darling Mummy, don't look so sad. Fiona doesn't mean half she says—'

But Fiona had fled. I think she thought that even she had gone too far this time.

When I got back from leaving the tickets at Mrs Musgrave's I found Fiona in a slightly better temper. She was in our joint bedroom, and her bed was covered with pairs of white tennis shorts and linen blouses. It appeared that David Eliot, one of the boys we had met at the Frazer's party, had rung up and asked us both to a tennis party at his home, Dewburn Hall. The Frazers would be there, and Guy Charlton, and quite a lot of other people we knew.

'It will be quite fun,' declared Fiona, holding up a pleated skirt and examining it critically. 'I wonder if I should wear a frock or shorts? They have a very nice court at Dewburn – not like that awful thing the Lister's have in their field. They call it a tennis court, but someone told me they made it themselves.'

'Well what if they did?' I argued. 'Home-made things are nearly always the best. Take cakes, for instance.'

'We aren't talking about cakes,' said Fiona. 'We're talking about tennis courts.'

'As a matter of fact, the Lister's court is a jolly nice one,' I persisted. 'It's ever so fast—'

'Oh, do shut up!' ordered Fiona. 'Really, Caroline, I don't know what's the matter with you. You do nothing but argue from morning till night!'

'Neither do you!' I snapped. 'Since you came home from school, there hasn't been a minute's peace—'

'Oh, so I'm to blame, am I?' stormed Fiona. 'I'm always to blame for everything! I expect you wish I was dead! Well, perhaps I *shall* die! I'm miserable enough!'

She dashed away in a proper tantrum, as Trixie would put it, and I was left to put away the clothes she'd left scattered all over the room.

Chapter 2

A Tennis Party

THERE were twelve people at the tennis party. Besides David Eliot, Fiona, and me, there were Guy Charlton, the boy who'd ridden part of the way home with us after the Frazers' party, Jane Foster, Nigel Monkhouse, Ian and Maud Frazer, two boys called Gordon and Dick, but I never found out what their surnames were, and two girls called June and Sylvia Dickson. We hadn't met them before. David's sister, Patience, wasn't allowed to play, because she'd been very ill after her mad prank at the Frazers' party.

Fiona had finally decided to wear a white silk shorts-frock, and she looked very lovely with her golden hair standing out round her face like a halo, and her blue eyes shining with excitement. I just wore shorts and a white Aertex shirt, because I felt it didn't really matter what I looked like – nobody would notice me when Fiona was there.

We drew for partners. I drew Ian Frazer, which didn't please me very much, because everyone knew he cheated. Fiona and Guy Charlton were partners; Maud and Gordon; Nigel and Sylvia; Jane and Dick; David and June. Patience Eliot perched herself on the top of a pair of steps beside the net, and said that she would be referee.

'OK. You can do it for half an hour or so,' David agreed. 'But not too long. You mustn't get tired. You know what Dr Henderson said.'

'Oh, I hate that horrible little man!' declared Patience, wrinkling up her nose. 'My pneumonia is quite all right now.'

It was a plain knockout tournament, because there wasn't time for the American sort, where everyone plays everyone else. I had an awful job with Ian Frazer, because he *would* keep on saying balls were in when they were out, and I'm afraid that Patience sometimes forgot her duties as referee, and nobody liked to tell her off on account of her pneumonia. I think that Fiona had an equally bad time with Guy, because, although she's my sister, I have to admit that sometimes Fiona doesn't play quite fair herself, and anyone could see from a glance at Guy's level grey eyes, that looked you straight in the face, that he'd rather die than cheat. Still, he was a wonderful player, and Fiona found that they won all their sets without her having to say a single ball was out when it wasn't!

'Wait till you meet Nigel and Sylvia!' teased David. 'They're the world's best tennis players, bar none! Sylvia's going to play on Wimbledon's centre court!'

Sylvia and Nigel were on the court at that moment, and I watched them critically. Yes, there was no doubt about it; they were frightfully good. Sylvia was a big, untidy girl with long, thin arms, and enormous feet. She padded about the court, like an outsize in panthers, and nothing seemed beyond her reach. She was certainly a good deal steadier than Fiona. The question was – did Nigel play as well as Guy? I thought not. For one thing, he was several years younger, and much smaller, and for another, he was rather erratic, whereas Guy was as steady as a rock. Still, Sylvia . . .

'Yes, she's tremendous, isn't she?' David said, following my gaze. 'I shouldn't wonder if, as I said before, she doesn't end up at Wimbledon! She's got the temperament. Nothing like tennis stars for temperament! I've heard Sylvia can't play with any racket except that old one she's playing with now, and it's certainly a most peculiar shape. Poor old Sylvia! It must be a great responsibility keeping it safe!'

'I never heard anything so silly!' exclaimed Fiona. 'I expect she'd play ten times better with a Slazenger.'

'I expect she wouldn't,' I laughed. 'Superstition is a funny thing. You know my cousin, Veronica – the one who's at Sadler's Wells? Well, she has an ancient pair of ballet shoes belonging to Madame somebody or other who was once a great dancer, and she takes them simply everywhere with her. She thinks they bring her luck! They stay in her dressing-room while she dances, and I wouldn't mind betting she takes them to bed with her at night! I believe, if she went to America they'd go with her – in the *Queen Mary*!'

'I'm pretty sure they would!' laughed little Jane Foster. 'Mummy's sister, my Aunt Irma, is a famous dancer, and she has two swan feathers, that she says once belonged to Anna Pavlova, sewn into the bodice of her Swan Queen costume. When she has a new costume made, they have to be taken out of the old one, and sewn into the new! I wonder what the dressmakers think?'

'Oh, I expect they get used to dealing with temperamental people!' I laughed.

'Gosh! Isn't it hot!' put in David. 'Let's stop for a breather after this set, shall we? Lemonade anyone?'

I'm afraid some of us were highly inelegant and drank our lemonade sitting on the edge of the burn that flows through the Eliots' garden. It's called the Dew Burn, and that was how Dewburn Hall got its name.

Fiona sat well away from the edge on Guy's sweater, looking very superior, and being careful to keep away from the people who splashed.

'Lemonade, Sylvia?' yelled David. 'Golly! Don't say you two have won another set?'

'Yes – six-two,' said Nigel, adding generously: 'Mostly won by Sylvia, I'm afraid. The games we lost were my services.' Nigel Monkhouse was a very queer boy, I decided. If you could *do* things, he admired you openly; if you couldn't, he despised you – openly, also! Poor Jane, his cousin, came in for a lot of acid remarks about her tennis, which certainly wasn't up to much. Jane was a bit of a puzzle, too. She was, as I've just said, a 'rabbit' at tennis, didn't like riding, wasn't much use, so she confessed, at swimming, and she didn't care for sports. It was difficult to find out what she *did* like.

Yet I couldn't help feeling that she was an awfully nice girl.

I was thinking about Jane when Sylvia dashed up.

'Oh, what a good idea!' she exclaimed, flopping down beside us and running a hand through her unruly hair, incidentally making it more unruly than ever. 'Can I dabble, too?'

'Who's to play next?' David asked, looking at the score sheet. 'Guy, what about you and Fiona?'

'I'm ready,' Guy said, standing up. 'But we seem to have played everybody except Maud and Gordon, and Maud's gone up to the house for something. Then, of course, there's Sylvia and Nigel, but they've just come off. Would it be too much for you to play again straight away, Sylvia?'

'Oh, no. I'm OK,' Sylvia said, jumping up too. 'I can dabble after we've beaten you! Where my racket?'

There was a sudden splash, and a cry from Fiona.

'Oh, Sylvia! I'm so frightfully sorry!'

'What's the matter? Oh, no! Not – *not* my racket!'

We all dashed to the edge of the burn, and our worst fears were realized. There, floating down the stream, was Sylvia's precious racket – the one and only racket she could play with.

Before anyone could do anything, Guy had torn off his tennis shoes, lowered himself into the stream, and was wading towards it. But he was too late. The stream flowed into a culvert at the end of the lawn, and Sylvia's racket floated merrily down a few little rapids and disappeared in the yawning pipe before our horrified eyes.

Of course, we all rushed to the other end of the culvert, which was in a little wood outside the Eliot's garden. We waited and waited, watching the outlet like cats at a mouse-hole, hoping against hope that the racket would come out again. But the minutes passed and it didn't appear. It was awful!

'I'm afraid it must have stuck,' came Fiona's voice, and there was a triumphant sound in it. 'I'm so *frightfully* sorry, Sylvia. I just can't *think* what happened, or how I could have been so careless. Of course, you must have mine. It's a very expensive one – a Slazenger.'

'But I can't play with yours,' said Sylvia, stamping her foot and tossing back her wild hair. 'I don't care if it's the most expensive racket that was ever made. I can't play with *any* racket except my own.'

'Well, that's just too bad,' said Fiona smoothly. 'But, of course, it couldn't be helped, could it? I mean, you leaving your racket right on the edge of the stream like that and it falling in. Accidents will happen.'

Well, it *might* have been an accident, of course, but knowing Fiona, I, for one, wasn't at all sure; and neither, I could see, was Guy. He stared at Fiona with a very queer expression in his grey eyes.

Now the strange thing was that Guy, as I have said before, was a magnificent tennis player – strong and steady. Yet during the game that followed, he was really most erratic. His balls went into the net, he served double faults at crucial moments in the game, he sent more than one 'skyscraper' that went sailing right over the top of the Eliots' summer-house and gave the game to the opposing side. In fact, you might almost have said he tried his level best to lose the set!

Fiona was furious.

'I do think you ought to remember I'm here,' she grumbled, when Guy poached flagrantly and lost the point. 'I could have reached that ball perfectly well. In fact, I was a lot nearer to it than you were.'

'Sorry!' apologized Guy. 'I ought to have got it all right, but my racket slipped. It was an accident. Accidents will happen you know! Serving to you, Nigel. Score is love-thirty. Oh, I'm *so* sorry!' This was after a double fault. 'The score is now love-forty. Where's Patience? She's supposed to be umpiring! Serving to you, Sylvia. Another double fault. I do apologize, Fiona! I seem to have completely lost my form. Well, that's the set. Six to you, Nigel; three to us. Congratulations, both of you!'

At this moment there was a sudden diversion. A dripping wet object appeared from the direction of the burn – an object holding to her breast Sylvia's lost tennis racket!

'Patience!' yelled the horrified David. 'Patience! Your pneumonia—'

'It's all right!' panted the figure. 'I've got it! I crawled through the pipe, and there it was – stuck right in the very middle! I was just small enough. It was a bit of a squeeze, but there you arc, Sylvia – your racket!' She held out the wet racket to the astonished Sylvia, who clutched it as if it was a long-lost child. 'Don't *fuss*, David! I'm perfectly warm. Feel me!' She thrust one small, wet hand against David's cheek, leaving behind a muddy smear. 'It's OK. I took off my shorts and my blouse before I went in, so old Hollingworth won't be too livid!'

'You must go straight up to the house,' ordered David, 'and have a hot bath.'

'Oh, David! Not a *hot* bath,' pleaded Patience. 'On a lurid day like this! A cold bath would get me just as clean. It would, honestly!'

'A *hot* bath,' persisted David. 'It's not cleanliness I'm thinking about, though you *are* pretty filthy. It's your pneumonia. You know—'

'What Dr Henderson said!' chanted Patience. 'OK. I'll have a hot bath if it'll make you happy, but if I melt away and go floating down the plug-hole as a spot of grease, *you'll* have to crawl down after me, David! I shan't be there to do it for myself!'

Chapter 3

Mostly about Lady Blantosh

AFTER these happenings, everything went smoothly for a bit. We had tea, and David saw that Patience had her hot bath. Then we all went down to the court again to see Maud and Gordon play Dick and Jane. Ian and I were out of it, having been beaten by Guy and Fiona earlier in the afternoon, and the latter were out because they'd been beaten by Nigel and Sylvia. Guy offered cheerfully to look for balls in the shrubbery, a thankless task, because no sooner had you found one than another one would be sure to go and bury itself in the thickest and most inaccessible spot. Fiona sat on a garden-seat, trying not to look sulky about being beaten because Ian was there. Most of the others were dabbling their feet in the burn.

Presently I heard voices and, looking round, I saw Mrs Hollingworth, the Eliots' housekeeper, approaching with someone in tow.

'It's that frightful Lady Blantosh,' said Fiona. 'I wonder what she wants?'

Personally, I didn't think Lady Blantosh frightful a bit, especially after what she'd said about me being slimmer. Of course, she did squint and wear queer clothes, but she was very kind-hearted, and I expect she did more good than many beautifully-dressed people who looked at you with both eyes at once. When she got near the court, she looked round it with her short-sighted eyes, and said anxiously: 'I wonder if little Jane Foster is here? I was told I should find her playing tennis.'

'She's on the court, Lady Blantosh,' Fiona volunteered. 'This is the final set. Shall I get her for you?'

Lady Blantosh peered at the court.

'Oh, no – don't disturb her now, especially if this is the finals. I was just wondering about the entertainment I'm getting up for my orphan children, you know. It's to be a play – a shortened form of *A Midsummer Night's Dream*, and I want someone for Titania. It must be someone graceful, with a nice-speaking voice. I thought little Jane would do splendidly.'

'Oh!—' I could tell by the sound of her voice that Fiona was jealous. I knew she'd often fancied herself as Titania, but at school everyone knew Fiona too well to choose her for the part, because she was far too lazy to learn her lines.

'We're having one or two other items,' went on Lady Blantosh. 'A couple of Spanish dances by a very talented young man. He's Spanish, but his people live in England, and I think he's coming up to the University in the Michaelmas term. His name is—'

'Angelo Ibañez!' I shrieked.

'Then you know him?'

'Oh, yes,' I said. 'He's a very great friend of Sebastian's. He wanted me to be his partner, but, of course, I'm rather young. I haven't seen Angelo since the Frazer's party at Christmas. I wonder how he's getting on, and if he's managed to get a partner.'

'Yes, a girl called Margarita,' said Lady Blantosh. 'I don't think she's Spanish, though she certainly looks it. I think her real name is Marjorie Manners; but, of course, Margarita sounds better. I think she must be a good deal older than you, Caroline, though she isn't any bigger. She's a charming little thing, with such lovely manners. I always think her surname most appropriate. Well, besides the Spanish dancers, we're hoping that dear Sebastian will be home from London, and will play for us.'

'Oh, that would be lovely!' I exclaimed. 'I *do* hope it comes off. I'm dying to see Sebastian again. It seems years and years since he went away, although I know it's only months.'

At this point Mrs Hollingworth broke in to ask if we wanted

the ice-cream sent down here, or if we'd go up to the house for it.

'Down here, please!' yelled David, who happened to have heard what she said. 'Shall I come and help cart it?'

Mrs Hollingworth said no, she'd get Ebenezer, the Eliots' old gardener, to wheel it down on the water-barrow.

Meanwhile the four finalists on the tennis court looked as if they were going on for ever.

'Seven all!' yelled David, who was now acting as referee. 'Your service, Gordon!'

'Oh, dear! I don't quite know what to do,' said Lady Blantosh. 'I hate to break up the set. I know enough about tennis to know you can't break off in the middle, but—'

'If you're in a hurry, I'll give Jane a message for you,' offered Fiona, favouring Lady Blantosh with a dazzling smile, so dazzling that I wondered what was afoot. 'I'll tell her you want her to be Titania, and she can ring you up tonight.'

'Oh, that would do splendidly,' said Lady Blantosh. 'How extremely kind of you, Fiona! If you would do that, then I can dash away to my committee meeting. Goodbye, all of you! *Goodbye!*'

She waddled away on her high-heeled shoes, and Mrs Hollingworth went with her to see about the ice-cream. We watched the two of them walk together towards the house; then Lady Blantosh turned off at the terrace, and set off down the drive. She always drove herself in her little sports car, but she usually left it at the bottom of people's drives because she feared it might be difficult to turn at the top!

Suddenly Fiona sprang up from the garden seat.

'Oh, I've forgotten something! Never mind, I'll dash after her.' She sped away, and we saw her catch up with Lady Blantosh and talk to her; but of course, we were too far away to hear what it was she said. In a few minutes she was back again.

'I forgot to ask her when the show was,' she panted. 'Stupid of me! Oh, and by the way, she doesn't want Jane to do it, after all. Guess what? She wants *me*! She said she changed her mind when she saw me looking so like a fairy queen.'

'Well, of course, you certainly *look* the part,' I said doubtfully, 'but do you think you'll ever learn it, Fiona? At school you—'

'Oh, do be quiet, Caroline!' ordered Fiona, turning red. 'Of course I shall learn it. I've never had a decent part before – that's why I haven't learnt them. It's no use trying to learn silly little parts. Now *this* will be wonderful!' She struck an attitude:

' "How sweet the moonlight sleeps upon this bank.
Here will we sit and let the sounds of music
Creep in our ears."

'You see, I can do it perfectly!'

'Yes, but there's an awful lot more to learn than just that well-known bit,' I said. 'And anyway, that's not in *A Midsummer Night's Dream*; it's in *The Merchant of Venice*.'

'Oh, shut up!' said Fiona again. 'I've *said* I'll learn it, haven't I?'

The tennis party finished at seven o'clock, and we all went home by ones and twos. Jane and Nigel had ridden over, so they went back on their ponies. Ian and Maud went home by car, taking Dick, Gordon, Sylvia, and June. Fiona and I had walked over to Dewburn Hall, as it's only about three miles across the moor, and it was such a lovely day. It had been pretty hot coming, but going back in the cool of the evening it was lovely.

Our way lay across open moorland as far as the telephone kiosk; then along the country road for about a mile, then across two fields, after which we were within sight of Bracken Hall.

When we got to the kiosk, I couldn't help remembering how it had looked when we'd reached it that day last winter, when

Veronica, Sebastian, and I had been lost in the storm. On that occasion it had been half buried in snow, with the wind whistling round it, and the drifts growing deeper every minute. Today, it stood on the wide grass verge, knee-deep in meadowsweet and clover. The smell of melting tar on the country road mingled pleasantly with the scent of honeysuckle and bedstraw in the hedgerow.

I was just about to remark to Fiona how much greater the contrasts are in the country between winter and summer – quite different to the town where the seasons all seem much the same, when we heard the sound of a pony's hooves thudding on the turf behind us.

'Oh, it's Guy!' I exclaimed. 'Hullo, Guy! We thought you'd gone home ages ago.'

'No, I had to change,' he said. 'Couldn't ride home decked out in white flannels!'

'But I didn't know this was in your direction?' I said. 'In fact, I thought you went exactly the other way.'

'I do, as a matter of fact,' he answered. 'I really followed you because I wanted to talk to you – you, Fiona.'

'Me?' Fiona didn't sound very pleased at this pronouncement. 'Well, I don't see why you couldn't have talked to me before – at the tennis party. We've had all the afternoon—'

'You see—' Guy hesitated, and sounded a little uncomfortable. 'You see – I feel I'd rather do it with no one else there. In private, I mean. Oh!' he added hastily. 'I didn't mean you, Caroline. In fact, you may be able to explain matters, as Fiona's your sister. You see—' He hesitated again and then went on firmly: 'You see, Fiona, I heard you talking to Lady Blantosh in the drive.'

'Well?' said Fiona. 'What about it?'

'I didn't mean to eavesdrop,' explained Guy, 'but I didn't know there was anything I ought not to hear—'

'There wasn't,' said Fiona flatly.

'Oh, then that's all right,' said Guy. 'I heard you tell Lady Blantosh that you'd given her message to Jane Foster and asked her if she wanted to be Titania in the show at the end of the holidays, and that Jane said she didn't.'

'That's right,' agreed Fiona.

'Oh, but Fiona—' I broke in.

'You shut up, Caroline!' ordered Fiona. 'This is my affair.'

'And mine, too,' said Guy, 'seeing that I overheard.'

'If Jane doesn't want the part, I can't help it, can I?' said Fiona. 'I just offered to help Lady Blantosh by saying I'd do it myself. Nothing wrong in that, I hope?'

'Just one small matter,' said Guy, stroking his pony's nose thoughtfully with his riding-crop. 'I happened to be fagging balls for Jane and Nigel all the time they were playing. I know for a fact you never asked Jane anything. She had no idea that Lady Blantosh had offered her the part for the simple reason that you never told her. I know that, Fiona.'

Fiona's face grew red, and she didn't reply.

'Well?' said Guy.

'I wish you'd mind your own business!' she said at length. 'You've never liked me, Guy Charlton. You've always had your knife into me, though I haven't the least idea what for. At that tournament you made me lose the prize, and it was something I've always wanted – a real anti-dazzle eye-shield. I think you're detestable! Perfectly detestable!'

'We'll leave your feelings for me out of it, if you don't mind,' Guy said coldly. 'The question now is whether what I suspect is true. Did you, or did you not, tell Jane about the play?'

'As you know so much, you may as well know the rest,' said Fiona. 'No, I didn't tell her. Why should I do Lady Blantosh's errands for her? Why can't the old hag do her own dirty work?'

'Oh, Fiona!' I exclaimed. 'You *offered* to tell Jane; you know you did!'

Fiona said nothing to this, merely shrugging her shoulders as if she didn't care.

'Well, now we've got to the bottom of it,' Guy said, 'we'd

better go back to the kiosk, hadn't we? You must tell Lady Blantosh you've changed your mind and can't take the part.'

Fiona stared at him.

'I shall do no such thing!'

'Oh, yes you will.'

'I will not!'

Guy passed his pony's reins to me, and advanced upon Fiona purposefully. As for Fiona, she took one look at his resolute face and gave in. Together we walked back to the kiosk. Guy taking his pony back from me and leading him, and Fiona's face growing darker every minute.

We reached the kiosk, and Guy opened the door.

'Go on, Fiona! Her number's Dewburn 1.' Then, as Fiona made no move to obey him, he added to no one in particular: 'You know, I've lived on a ranch in Canada most of my life, and when I came back to this country it seemed funny to me the way girls are treated as sort of sacred in England. No matter what they do, they don't get beaten. I feel like forgetting it, now and again! You'd better get that telephoning done, Fiona, or this might really be the time!'

Fiona turned scarlet.

'You wouldn't dare!'

'Oh, wouldn't I?' He dialled Lady Blantosh's number, and silently handed the receiver over to Fiona. In a very few seconds we heard Lady Blantosh's kind voice at the other end.

'This is Fiona Scott,' said Fiona sulkily.

'Oh, hullo, dear!' said the voice at the other end. 'How nice of you to ring me up!'

'Go on! Say you can't do it,' prompted Guy.

'I—' began Fiona. 'I can't—'

'What's that, dear? Speak up! You can't *what*?'

'Be quick! We can't wait here all day!' said Guy in her ear. 'Tell her you can't do it.'

'I—' said Fiona again, and stopped.

Guy took his riding-crop from under his arm, and looked from it to Fiona.

'I can't be Titania,' said Fiona very quickly.

'Tell her Jane will be pleased to do it, you expect,' prompted Guy. 'Go on! Say you'll be seeing Jane and you'll ask her.'

'Jane will do it,' repeated Fiona.

'Oh, so she's changed her mind, dear child,' said Lady Blantosh at the other end of the wire. 'How very sweet of her! But what about you, Fiona, darling?'

'I – I don't want to do it, now,' said Fiona, looking at Guy nervously from under her eyelashes. 'No, really, Lady Blantish, I couldn't do it, now.'

'Jane will do it ever so much better,' prompted Guy.

Poor Fiona repeated the words, and Lady Blantosh gurgled blissfully at the other end.

'Oh, well – as long as *one* of you does it. And now I really must fly! So nice of you to ring me up! Goodbye!'

'Goodbye!' said Fiona, jamming down the receiver savagely. She turned upon Guy in a fury. '*Now* I suppose you're happy! *Now* I suppose you think you've done a fine thing! Well, I hope you're satisfied!'

'Very!' said Guy. 'I think that justice has been done – at least as far as Jane is concerned. As far as *you're* concerned, Fiona, I still think that what you need is – oh, well – never mind!'

Fiona didn't answer. She dashed away over the heather without a word to either of us.

'Don't forget you've got to let Jane know about the part!' Guy yelled after her.

After she had disappeared, I'm afraid I collapsed on a tuft of heather and put my head in my hands.

'Caroline—' Guy said, sounding quite alarmed.

I looked up at him. Then I began to giggle.

'I'm not crying. I'm laughing!'

Then Guy began to laugh too.

'Golly! The sight of you with that riding-crop!' I said when I could speak. 'Poor Fiona!'

'What I'd have given to use it on her! exclaimed Guy. 'Gosh! The things some girls can do and get away with! It amazes me! Well, I'd better be making tracks, I suppose. It's been a grand party, in spite of the little to-do at the end. So long, Caroline!'

He swung himself into the saddle and rode off across the moor, leaving me to follow in the wake of my wrathful sister.

The Second Year

Winter

Chapter 1

I Discuss My Plan

SUMMER passed very quickly. Apart from Lady Blantosh's concert when Sebastian came from London for a couple of thrilling days and I met Angelo again, nothing very exciting happened. Angelo hadn't come up to the University, after all, so I was more lonely than ever. Before we knew where we were, the leaves had fallen from the trees, the last swallow had vanished, the days had shortened until they became almost like one long twilight, and suddenly Christmas had come and gone.

One day in February I got a letter from Veronica.

> Dear Caroline [it said]. Today was one of the most thrilling of my life. I'm actually a member of the Second Company! Beg its pardon, I should say the Theatre Ballet, to give it its proper name! Yes, I really am! The ballet mistress from down at the Wells came to class this morning and chose four of us – June, Delia, Denise (who's a particular friend of mine. She's French, as I expect you can guess by her name!) and me. It's so wonderful that I can hardly believe it even yet, though it's eleven o'clock at night – twelve whole hours from the moment I was told. Surely if it was a dream I'd have wakened up by now, shouldn't I?
>
> Oh, and I forgot to tell you, we're going on tour – Vienna, Helsinki, Rome, perhaps, and Portugal. We finish

in Paris! After that, there's some talk about an American tour, so I'm afraid it'll be ages before I see you all again. I'll be thinking about you, though! I shall never forget Bracken Hall with its fir woods, and the lovely cool moors where the wind always blows, no matter how stifling it is everywhere else. When I'm in some outrageously hot city, I shall think of the bracken growing shoulder-high, and the curlews wheeling, and the larks – 'linties' as they call them on the Border – singing their heads off in the misty blue air. I don't think even Italy could possibly be as beautiful as Bracken in the spring!

I'm afraid this is a very short letter, but I've such lots to do before I can go to bed, and it's now eleven-thirty! There are my tights to wash, and a new pair of point shoes to finish darning. Rehearsals for *The Gods Go A-Begging* start to-morrow, and I *think* I'm going to be a Black Lackey. Imagine it! How I used to envy Belinda Beaucaire when she got that part! She's dancing the principal part now, by the way – the Serving-maid.

Well, I really must stop now. Lots of love to everybody, not forgetting dear Trixie, and the ponies (give Arabesque a special kiss for me), and Pharaoh, my darling cat.

VERONICA

PS – My letters always have a PS, haven't they! Delia says her brother, who's at the Royal College of Music, knows Sebastian quite well. She says Maurice – that's her brother's name – says Sebastian is very highly thought of at the RCM. The high-ups consider him one of the most brilliant students the College has ever had. Maurice thinks he'll get an Exhibition to study abroad – a place with a funny name where Eileen Joyce went. Do you ever hear from him, Caroline? Sebastian, I mean? I've never had a single word from him since I left Northumberland and we had that awful quarrel. Once I *thought* I saw him at a concert at the Albert Hall, but there were such hundreds of people in the way, I couldn't get near. Anyway, I expect it was someone else with black hair!

I do wish Sebastian – oh, never mind!

Love again,

VERONICA

I put the letter in my pocket, and went downstairs to tell Mummy about it, and suddenly I resolved to tell Mummy about my plan, too – the plan that had been simmering in my brain all through the winter.

I found Mummy in the dining-room, arranging Christmas roses in a low green glass bowl. Outside the long windows, the snow still lay thick and deep, though the strong sunlight made the room quite warm.

'Mummy,' I began, 'I wonder—'

'Oh, Caroline,' Mummy broke in, turning round, 'I want to talk to you about something rather important. You see—'

And then, all at once, Mummy was talking to me, saying the most helpful things, things that sounded almost as if she had guessed my great secret, which of course was impossible.

'You know, Caroline,' Mummy was saying, 'Daddy's business hasn't been doing well, lately. It's been a great strain to keep Fiona at her Harrogate school, and to manage all this' – her eyes strayed round the lovely room with its rich carpets and long velvet curtains. I was going to say 'the lovely warm room', but to be quite accurate it wasn't warm any more, because the central heating was only turned on when visitors came, and we'd got into the habit of having all our meals in the small breakfast-room.

'I'm afraid we shall have to economize pretty drastically,' Mummy went on. 'Cut the domestic staff, and so on. And there's this question of your school, Caroline. You were due to leave your Newcastle one next term, you know—'

'Oh, but Mummy,' I broke in excitedly, 'I don't want to go to a finishing school, like Fiona. I want to go to a *dancing* school.'

There was a dramatic pause.

'A *what* did you say?' gasped poor Mummy.

'A dancing school, Mummy,' I repeated.

'But you already go to one.'

'Oh, yes, I know, and it's a jolly good one, too,' I said. 'But what I mean is, I don't want to go away to a boarding school, like Fiona's. I want to go to Sadler's Wells. Oh, not the Senior part where Veronica went – I'm not good enough yet. I'm not old enough, either, as a matter of fact. You've got to be over fifteen. But they've got a Junior School, you know, where you learn everything. French, and Latin, and even maths – besides dancing. *That's* where I want to go, Mummy. Oh, *please*, Mummy! It wouldn't be nearly as expensive as a finishing school,' I added hastily, 'because you don't have to live there.'

'But you'd have to live *somewhere*,' argued Mummy.

'Oh, yes, of course, but Jane says – Jane Foster, I mean, Mummy. You know the Fosters who live at Monks Hollow? Well, Jane's aunt is the famous Irma Foster – she's a ballet dancer, and everybody's heard of her – and Mariella, who's Irma Foster's daughter and Jane's cousin, well, Mariella's training to be a dancer, and they live in London. I've talked to Jane about it, and she says I could live there, too, because Uncle Oscar is so absent-minded.'

Mummy held up her hands.

'Caroline! I don't know what in the world you're talking about! Who on earth is Uncle Oscar – *who's* uncle is he? – and what has his being absent-minded got to do with it?'

'He's Jane's uncle,' I explained, trying hard not to be impatient, 'and he's Irma Foster's husband, but don't let his being called Deveraux worry you. Jane says that famous people often have different names from their husbands. I mean, they go on using their maiden ones – the ones they had before they were married. Aunt Irma always uses hers, and Mariella uses it, too. That's why she's Mariella Foster, and not Deveraux.

Jane says they have a lovely flat in London – No 140*a* Fortnum Mansions, but poor Mariella is frightfully lonely because her mother's dancing all day long, and her father forgets all about her – so now you see where the absent-minded comes in? You see, he's a collector as well as a critic, and when he's collecting and cataloguing, he never even remembers he *has* a daughter! So you see, as Jane says, I'd be great company for Mariella.'

'And I suppose this Mariella goes to Sadler's Wells School?' said Mummy, looking a little more enlightened.

'Oh, no,' I said. 'She has a governess, and a tutor, because her mother – Irma Foster – has peculiar ideas. That's what Jane says. Jane says Mariella would miles rather go to a real school, but there you are. What can you do if your parents have peculiar ideas? And, after all, you can't have everything, can you?'

'Some people seem to have a very good idea about getting it,' Mummy said cryptically. 'I didn't know you were such friends with this Jane Foster. But since you are, and if her cousin, Mariella, really *is* lonely, perhaps we could arrange for you to stay there and share her governess. That would be quite a good idea—'

'Oh, no, Mummy, it wouldn't,' I broke in. 'Not to share Mariella's governess, I mean. It wouldn't be a good idea at all. It's all right for Mariella, because she doesn't go to the Wells School yet, though she does intend to go to the Senior School later on. But just now she goes to the Wakulski-Viret Dancing School.'

'Well, couldn't you go to the – to that school, too?' asked Mummy in that maddening way grown-ups have of assuming that one dancing school is just the same as another.

'Oh, *Mummy*!' I almost wailed. 'Don't you understand! I want to go to the *Wells*!'

'Well, couldn't you have lessons with Mariella, and go to the Wells for dancing?'

I shook my head.

'No, I couldn't. Not at my age. If I was over fifteen, I could go to the Senior School and be an Associate. Or if I was a teeny-weeny – not more than eleven – I could go to some other school, or share Mariella's lessons, and go to the Wells out-of-school classes. But at fourteen it has to be the Wells or nothing at all, if you see what I mean.'

'Oh, well—' said Mummy. 'We'll see what can be done. I suppose even the Wells School would be cheaper than the Harrogate one.'

'Oh, yes – miles and miles,' I assured her.

'I haven't yet found out how you got to know this Mariella,' said Mummy. 'I suppose she's been staying with Jane?'

'Yes, she stayed at Monks Hollow last summer,' I answered. 'And she was great fun. I liked her awfully. She learnt to ride in two shakes of a duck's tail, as Nigel put it – Nigel is Jane's cousin, too. Mariella was awfully keen on horses – not like Jane, who says she hates riding. I like Jane awfully, too, though of course she's quite different – much quieter. She goes to Miss Martin's dancing school, you know, and although she's only just started, she's getting on like a house on fire. I shouldn't wonder if *she* doesn't go to the Wells, too, later on. She'd like to, I know, but her people are such awful stick-in-the-muds.'

'Caroline!' exclaimed Mummy, shocked.

'Well, they *are*, Mummy,' I insisted. 'Sebastian says so.'

'Then of course they must be,' Mummy said with a smile, adding with a slight frown: 'But we shall have to go into this dancing business very carefully. Of course, you know that I don't really approve of dancing as a career – not for my daughter. I don't know what Daddy will think, either.'

'Oh, Mummy!' I wailed. 'You're talking like you did years ago – when Veronica first came from London to live with us. You know you've changed lots since then. Even Sebastian says so.'

Mummy didn't look as pleased as you might have expected at this statement. Sebastian was no favourite of hers. She had finished arranging the flowers by this time, and she gave a little shiver.

'Ugh! It's cold in here, in spite of the sun. Let's go into the breakfast-room and finish our talk in there – it's warmer. As I say, we shall have to go into it all most carefully. Just supposing you *did* go to the Wells School—' Mummy began piling logs on the breakfast-room fire. 'Supposing we *did* think about it, there's always Veronica. That Mrs Crapper she stays with—'

'Oh, no, Mummy!' I burst out. 'If I do go to London, I don't want Veronica to know – not until I make good. Besides, I've just had a letter from Veronica this very morning – that was what I wanted to tell you about, only you began about economizing. Well, Veronica's got into the Second Company, and she's going abroad, so she won't be at Mrs Crapper's any more, and I couldn't stay at Mrs Crapper's all by myself, could I? I mean, there wouldn't be any point in it, would there?'

'Not much,' agreed Mummy. To tell you the truth I don't think Mummy had ever really liked the idea of Mrs Crapper – not even for Veronica, let alone me.

'And anyway,' I argued, 'it would be frightfully silly, when Mariella is there at Fortnum Mansions being terribly lonely.'

'Of course, we should have to pay for you if you stayed with the Fosters, or the Deveraux – or whatever you call these people,' went on Mummy, half to herself.

'Oh, of course,' I agreed, 'But it wouldn't be much. They're disgustingly rich. Jane says so. She says money is simply no object with Uncle Oscar. And you see, I'd be doing them a good turn, really – being company for Mariella. The awful thing is,' I went on, 'I feel I shall never get accepted for the Wells School. You have to have an audition, you know – even for the Junior School – and it's *frightfully* stiff. You see, there are simply hundreds of children wanting to get in, and only places for a very few. So you've got to be most awfully good. I don't expect I shall stand an earthly—'

Chapter 2

Mariella

BUT this is where I was wrong. In the late spring, having talked Mummy and Daddy round, I went up to London for my audition, and was accepted for the school. I can't say they seemed frightfully impressed by my dancing, but they liked what they called my 'background', and I heard someone call me a 'graceful child, and musical too. And if she doesn't show promise later on, she can always go on to the teaching side. Really well-educated dancing teachers are always in great demand. We need them almost more than dancers.'

I don't know what Mummy thought about this pronouncement – Mummy had come up to London with me – because, although it was precisely what she had planned for Veronica, I'm pretty sure it wasn't at all what she had had in mind for me! However, she just smiled, and said she thought it would do me no harm for a year or two, since the school gave the pupils such a sound general education. In short, I left Colet Gardens enrolled as a member of the Sadler's Wells School.

I began there in the Easter term, and at first it was great fun. Afterwards – well, I shall be telling you about that later. At the present moment I must tell you a little about Fortnum Mansions, and Mariella. Mariella was pretty, with auburn hair and green eyes. As Jane had said, the Fosters had loads of money, and Mariella was used to just lifting up her little finger if she wanted anything, and hey presto! it dropped into her lap! I think she'd have been terribly astonished if it hadn't.

It was great fun staying with Mariella. For one thing, we were left very much to ourselves. Mariella's mother seemed to spend most of her life at the theatre, and when the ballet went on tour, she went with it. Whenever we saw her, she was kindness itself, and she was so lovely to look at I couldn't help staring at her. It wasn't only her creamy, pale, oval face, with its huge, sad dark eyes; it was the way she moved, and the graceful gestures of her hands. She seemed to talk with her hands, I thought.

'Your mother reminds me of someone, but I can't think who it is,' I said to Mariella one day when Irma Foster had had lunch with us between rehearsals.

'I know!' Mariella said, looking up from a book she was reading. 'It's my cousin, Jane. Jane is the very image of Mummy. And, as a matter of fact, I'm quite a bit like Jane's mother, Aunt Carol, myself. Funny, isn't it!'

'Yes,' I answered. 'What's that book you're reading, Mariella? It must be very interesting – you've never spoken all the afternoon.'

'Oh, it's a book about a pony,' Mariella said, holding it up. 'Jane gave it to me to read in the train after I'd been staying at Monks Hollow last summer. It's called *Wendy and Her Pony*, and it's the most wonderful book you ever read! You have a pony, haven't you, Caroline?'

'Yes – he's called Gillyflower,' I said.

'Well, don't you miss him frightfully?' asked Mariella.

I considered.

'As a matter of fact,' I said at length, 'I haven't had much time to miss anything since I came to London. We work pretty hard at the Wells, you know – all our school work, a dancing class before school, and another after, and then all our homework.'

Mariella nodded her bright head.

'Don't I know it! All those *battements*! Oh, for a real, full-out gallop! I'd give anything for a ride on an honest-to-goodness moor!'

'If you're so keen on it,' I said, 'wouldn't your people let you ride here?'

'In the Row, I suppose you mean – all dressed up!' said Mariella, making a naughty face. 'Complete with riding master to keep me in order! Mummy would be dead scared I fell off and broke something, and spoilt my wonderful career as a dancer. No, I don't want to ride *that* way, Caroline – thank you very much! I want to ride where it's free and open – not in mouldy old London!'

'By the way, Mariella, what does your father do all day?' I asked her, mainly to change the subject. 'I've hardly seen him since I came here.'

'Oh, he's got what I call a "jade spell" on,' explained Mariella. 'You know, Daddy collects jade. Well, last week he went to a sale and collected some, so now he's busy cataloguing it. He's so absent-minded when he's got a jade spell on that I don't believe he even recognizes *me*!'

'Oh, Mariella!' I said, half laughing.

'It's a fact. A few days ago he ran into Mummy in the hall, and she swears he looked at her and wondered who on earth she was!'

'I don't believe it!' I laughed.

It seemed queer to me that cataloguing a thing should take such a very long time, and make one so absent-minded, but Mariella assured me that it did.

'You see, Daddy's got to stare at each piece for hours together in order to decide whether it's Ming, or whatever it's supposed to be, and I expect after that everything and everybody he looks at looks like jade, so it's no wonder he doesn't recognize them!'

'Y-es, I see,' I answered, though I didn't really.

On the whole, No 140*a* Fortnum Mansions was quite a nice place to live in, though of course it wasn't like home. All our main meals were sent up in the lift from the restaurant, and you could order whatever you wanted. At first it was fun choosing, and it certainly saved a lot of trouble, but after a bit you got tired of it. As Mariella said, everything tasted the same as everything else. I couldn't help comparing the London meal of roast lamb and green peas and apple tart to follow, with Trixie's version of the same. Trixie's lamb would have potatoes roasted round it, and the peas would be freshly picked out of the kitchen garden, sweet and delicious. There would be freshly-made mint sauce – not just a gravy-boat full of vinegar with a sprinkling of mint floating on the top. Trixie's apple pie would be made with home-grown apples, and the pastry would be cooked on top of it. The London idea of an apple tart was a mound of stewed apple, with a square of pastry by the side of it. The two had obviously never met until the moment they were put on your plate, so no wonder they tasted insipid! Trixie's pie would be smothered with thick, yellow farm cream, instead of pale custard. Yes, I felt I'd appreciate Trixie's cooking, now, when I went home for the holidays!

Chapter 3

I See Veronica Dance

We often went to Covent Garden, because Uncle Oscar – I called him 'uncle' out of courtesy – had a box there, and he seldom wanted to go to a matinée, whereas naturally we weren't allowed to go out at night by ourselves. Sometimes we had to take Miss Linton, Mariella's governess, to the matinée, but sometimes Uncle Oscar said we could go alone, and then Miss Linton helped him with his cataloguing. The commissionaire at Covent Garden knew us, so Uncle Oscar knew we would come to no harm. I can't help thinking that Miss Linton preferred the cataloguing to going to the ballet with us.

Mariella had to get leave from her dancing school – the Wakulski-Viret one – to go, but she managed that easily enough, because everyone knows that watching a ballet performance is part of your education, especially if you're going to be a dancer. She had to produce the programme, though, to show she'd really been, whereas Saturdays were half-holidays for me at the Wells.

'Couldn't we have a change, and go to a performance at Sadler's Wells?' I said to Mariella one day after I'd been in London for several weeks. 'Someone at school told me that Veronica is in *Les Sylphides*. I'd love to see her.'

'OK,' Mariella said obligingly. I think she wasn't very keen about watching ballet, and only went so as to get out of her dancing lesson, and to please her mother, so she didn't really care which ballet she went to see.

We had a box at Sadler's Wells, too, and when the curtain rose on *Les Sylphides*, I was so excited I could hardly sit still.

'There she is!' I exclaimed in a whisper. 'The last one in

The curtain rose on Les Sylphides

the back row of the *corps de ballet*. That's Veronica!'

Mariella took her father's opera-glasses from the velvet ledge in front of her – she always borrowed them for these occasions – and studied Veronica critically.

'Yes, I've heard Daddy mention her,' she declared. 'He says she's worth watching, and when Daddy says that, it means something, I can tell you!'

For a long time I watched Veronica's movements, fascinated. Her small, pale oval face looked familiar, and yet not familiar. She had the same entranced expression as she had had when she'd danced this same dance at Lady Blantosh's concert all those years ago, and yet of course she was quite different. Her movements were now controlled, and what you might call 'finished'. Her dark eyes looked enormous; her slender arms were as graceful as the branches of a larch tree in spring. Her mouth was slightly open, and there was a wistful smile on her pale face. I knew that her thoughts were far away in the woods around my home, Bracken Hall, and that she was dancing not merely to earn her living, but because she loved it. Dancing was as natural to Veronica as the air she breathed, and as necessary.

'Oh, she's beautiful!' I said aloud. 'I shall never, never dance like Veronica!'

'No, I don't expect you ever will,' said Mariella more truthfully than diplomatically, I felt. 'Daddy's right, as usual. She *is* rather good.'

'Oh, and this is Belinda!' I exclaimed when the Waltz began. 'Belinda Beaucaire. Veronica's often told me about her. She's lovely, too, isn't she?'

'U-um – yes,' Mariella said. 'She's got red hair, like me, and green eyes, too, I shouldn't wonder! She's frightfully good technically, but I've heard Daddy say she'll never arrive.'

'Oh, why not?' I asked, leaning over the ledge of the box to get a better view. 'She looks marvellous to me.'

'She's too hard-bitten,' declared Mariella, copying the expression, I felt sure, from her father. I couldn't help thinking how horrified prim Miss Linton would have been if she could have heard it! 'She's got no soul. She's only dancing for what she can get out of it. She's – she's *common.* Yes, that just expresses it. Oh, I don't mean she's poor, or anything like that, or that she's got an awful Cockney accent and says "pleased to meet you", instead of "how d'you do". I just mean she isn't "nice". Oh, I know that's a stupid word, but it just describes Belinda Beaucaire. No, I put my shirt on your Veronica, even if she *is* at present in the back row of the *corps de ballet.* Daddy's never wrong.'

In the interval Mariella tried to persuade me to go round behind to tell Veronica I was here in London, but I wouldn't.

'No, I'd rather she didn't know. She's been so successful herself, you see, and if – if I wasn't—'

Mariella shrugged her shoulders expressively, a trick she had caught from her mother.

'Oh, well – have it your own way! It seems queer to me, though. If you aren't a success, you can go back home, and really why you ever left that lovely place in Northumberland, Caroline, I can't think. You must be bats!'

When the curtain went up on *The Gods Go A-Begging*, I looked again for Veronica. It was harder this time. Trying to pick out one Black Lackey from among the rest was almost impossible.

'All exactly the same,' pronounced Mariella.

'Oh, no – that's Veronica by herself at the back of the stage.'

'Glad you recognize her!' Mariella said sarcastically. 'I'll take your word for it! Here comes Belinda as the Serving-maid. She certainly dances well, but watch her expression. She's got what Daddy calls a "never-fading smile"!'

'Yes, I see what you mean,' I answered. 'All the same, she *is* wonderful – so beautifully graceful, and so lovely to look at with that red-gold hair.'

'There's much more to ballet than just being graceful and having wonderful red hair,' declared Mariella. 'But I agree –

she's talented, and it's a dreadful waste.' Again I felt she was copying her father when she said this.

Belinda looked her most exquisite at the end of the ballet when she stood on her pedestal at the back of the stage. She did indeed look a goddess! It was hard to believe that Oscar Deveraux's criticism of her could be correct.

After the show we stopped for a moment outside the theatre to look at the photographs. Crowds of people were surging out of the doors from the cheaper seats. I caught a fleeting glimpse of a closely-cropped black head.

'Sebastian! Wait for me, Sebastian! Oh – he's gone!'

'Friend of yours?' inquired Mariella sympathetically.

'Yes – Sebastian Scott, my cousin. You remember I told you about him. He's in London, too, studying music. I wanted so much to see him and ask him to the flat. He'd love the flat with Aunt Irma's Steinway piano.'

'Well, he's gone now,' said Mariella. 'He seemed in an awful hurry. Can't you find out his address from someone?'

'Oh, yes, of course. I should have done it ages ago. It'll mean writing to Uncle Adrian, though – that's Sebastian's father, you know – and I hate writing letters to grown-ups, except Mummy and Daddy, of course. Besides, I have an idea Sebastian may be going abroad to study soon. In fact, I thought he'd already gone. Oh, why couldn't he have waited!'

'I expect he would if he'd seen you,' said Mariella sensibly. 'Oh, well, it can't be helped. Here's our bus. Come on, Caroline. I want some tea, if you don't!'

As we wound our way homeward in the bus through London's traffic, my thoughts went back to Sebastian. It was obvious he'd been to Sadler's Wells to see Veronica dance. I wondered if he had repented of his quarrel with her? Surely he wouldn't go to see her dance if he was still furious with her? But Sebastian was such a queer boy that I wasn't at all sure what he would do.

Chapter 4

My First Day at the Wells

USUALLY one's first day at a new school is exciting, and perhaps a little terrifying. There are all the strange people, and the building is unfamiliar, things are done in an entirely different way from the way you've been used to doing them before, and altogether you feel rather like a fish out of water! Imagine, then, not only a new school, but a ballet school at that! People running about in tights and tunics; exciting sounds of a piano playing ballet music; people talking 'shop', by which I mean talk about the latest ballets seen from the inside. Snatches of conversation from the students' dressing-room reached me:

'Oh, my dear, did you see Belinda in *The Gods*? Wasn't it awful? That *smile*! Reminded me of the toothpaste advert – "Have you cleaned your teeth today with *Dazzle*? You bet I have!" Someone ought to tell her to tone it down a bit!'... 'Veronica Weston's coming on, they say. Someone saw her the other night as Ecossaise in *Façade*. Said she was good. I always said—' ... 'Heard the latest rumour? Oh, yes, they say Marcia Rutherford's got the leading part in *Dance for Poppa*! Principal's got appendix, or something. Some people have all the luck! But of course it may not be *all* luck. Trust Marcia to get in with the producers! She *would*!' ... 'Thank goodness she's out of ballet proper. Can't stand the thought of that girl degrading the art!'...

But to get back to the beginning, Mariella and Miss Linton took me as far as the door of the school, but I refused to let them come in with me because I didn't want to appear babyish. Miss Linton seemed rather relieved – I think the very idea of a ballet school terrified her. Or perhaps she didn't feel it was altogether decent! Anyway, she heaved a sigh of relief when I said I'd be quite all right now, thank you, and she and Mariella could go home.

'Well, if you're quite sure, dear—'

'Oh, yes, I'd much rather go by myself,' I assured her.

Mariella, on the other hand, wanted to come in with me and see everything.

'After all, I shall be coming here myself some day,' she said, 'if they'll have me.' Then she added under her breath: 'Sometimes I rather hope they won't. Dancing with Maestro is bad enough, but I have an idea this place will be even worse! Oh, well – if you won't let me come in with you, Caroline, I suppose you won't. I must say, though, I'd have liked to see the lions feeding!'

'But they won't be feeding!' I laughed. 'It's early morning.'

'I expect they feed all day long,' said Mariella in a sepulchral whisper. 'On their victims' blood! Oh, all right, Caroline, I'll be there to welcome you when you come out of the lions' den – if you ever *do* come out – alive!'

With that she was gone, leaping after her long-suffering governess like a graceful young antelope. I must admit that Mariella's ballet classses had at least made her graceful, however much she hated them. She never looked awkward, even when she was doing the most uninspiring things, like, for instance, fastening up her back suspenders, or zipping up the back of her frock.

I found the school in a state of great excitement. It appeared that the studios were full of film people with their cameras and other equipment. They were here to take shots of Sadler's Wells at work.

'They're busy with the senior ballet students now,' said a girl whose peg was next to mine in the dressing-room. 'So they won't get down to us till after school. Gilbert will be in a rare bad temper by then! By the way, you're new, aren't you? Name?'

'Caroline Scott,' I answered. 'Yes, I'm new. Who do you mean by Gilbert?'

'Thank goodness!' said the girl. 'Oh, I didn't mean for Gilbert, though he *is* a lamb when he's in a good mood. I mean, your name being Caroline. We'd have kicked you out if you'd been June!'

'Why?' I asked.

'There are seven Junes in the Junior School – that's why! Another would have just about finished us off!'

'As a matter of fact my mother's name is June,' I said shamefacedly. 'And I expect I'd have been June, too, but my birthday happens to be in November. What's *your* name?'

'June!' said the girl, with a grin. 'June Turnbull. I'm one of the seven! They call us the Seven Deadly Sins, and there's a poem somebody made up about us called *We are seven*. It's a parody on a poem composed by somebody or other and it's rather funny – our version, I mean. What was I saying?'

'You were talking about Gilbert,' I prompted. 'Do you mean Gilbert Delahaye – the temperamental ballet master?'

'Yes, of course. The one and only Gilbert!' laughed June. 'Do you know him? You sound as if you do. I thought you said you were new?'

'Yes, I am,' I told her. 'But Veronica told me all about Gilbert.'

'You mean, Veronica Weston?' said June with interest. 'Fancy you knowing her! She was a big noise here. Oh, I don't mean she was actually rowdy – matter of fact she was most awfully quiet and modest – but she was thought no end of by Gilbert, and Madame, and all the high-ups. A sort of Margot Fonteyn! We all think Veronica is out to hit the sky! Is she really a friend of yours?'

'She's my cousin,' I said.

I hadn't meant to cause a sensation, but I certainly did it. The dressing-room was all agog.

'Goodness! What an honour! You'll be able to have her for your mascot.'

'What's that?' I asked.

'Well, it's a dancer you adore in the Company,' explained June. 'You send flowers to her, and so on. She hands down her old ballet shoes to you – if you're lucky. Mary Duncan chose Belinda Beaucaire for hers, though, and she's never had a pair yet, so it just shows! But you ought to be all right with your cousin, Veronica. Why, you might even get one of her old *tutus* to wear in the *pas de deux* class, if you ever get into it – the class, I mean. You've got to be terribly good.'

'You were telling me about a film they're taking of the Seniors,' I prompted her again. She seemed an awful girl for not sticking to the point.

'Oh, yes. Well, June Campbell – June No Two – sneaked up to the Baylis Hall and hid in the balcony, and she says it was priceless! There were all the film people cluttering up the place, and Gilbert in the middle of the mess, roaming up and down like a caged tiger, stepping over cameras, and ropes, and people's coats, and goodness knows what else, and looking as if he'd explode any minute. Finally he did – explode, I mean! He told the film people he supposed they could take their old film if, as they said, they'd got permission – *he* couldn't stop them! But just let him catch them taking one shot of *him*, said Gilbert; just let him catch them recording one single word of *his*, growled Gilbert, and he'd kick them out into Colet Gardens – cameras, microphones, sweaters, and all! Neck and crop, spat Gilbert! Then he went on striding up and down, talking all the time, and getting in the way of the cameras, whenever the poor film men tried to take a shot of the class. June said it was enough to make a cat laugh! Finally, they found it was quite impossible to get in a shot when he wasn't there and wasn't talking, and they went away in disgust. Some of the Seniors were furious, but Gilbert wouldn't care about that. He's very modest himself, and he expects everyone else to be modest, too. Films aren't much in Gilbert's line.'

'He sounds rather nice,' I commented.

'Oh, he's a lamb, as I said before,' declared June. 'Except when he's in a rage, that is. Then he ought to be labelled: "DANGEROUS! This animal bites!" – like the zoo!'

'Look here – oughtn't I to be going somewhere?' I asked. 'I mean, isn't there a class or something?'

'Oh, you mean *lessons*?' a girl, who evidently owned the peg on the other side of me, said, as if she'd never heard of the word. 'Yes, there is. It's English first period on Mondays. But today is the beginning of the term and we never do much except make out timetables, and get ourselves generally sorted out. You know, I suppose, that our ballet class comes first usually, but it's been put off today because of the film people. That's something else that annoys Gilbert. He says: "Work, with a capital W, should come before everything – even such important and world-shattering things as films!" I have an idea he's being sarcastic.'

'By the way, this is Frizzle,' said my new friend, June, indicating a very fair girl on the other side of the dressing-room. 'I think you're in her form, New Girl. I should say Caroline. Oh, yes, it's by way of being a funny name, isn't it? It usually startles people, but we've all got used to it now. Her real name's Thelma Thistlethwaite.'

'Then why?—' I began.

'Oh, it was Serge Lopokoff,' broke in June. 'He's the Character master, you know, and he's Russian to the core. His English is Russian to the core, too! In other words, he doesn't like the English, so he simply can't get round their language, and he doesn't try too much – especially the "th"s. Well, when he met Thelma Thistlethwaite, he'd met his Waterloo! He got it to Felmer Fisselfaite, but even that was too much for him, and he finally shortened it to Fizzle, and she's been that ever since! Usually,' added June candidly, 'old Serge doesn't bother about all our names – he just calls us "you", which is about the one and only English word he knows, but you see Thelma happens to be really good, especially at Character, so he made the effort. Poor Fizzle!'

Personally, I didn't think Fizzle looked at all depressed, in spite of the mess the Russian dancing master had made of her name. She was very pretty with naturally curly hair and a lovely smile.

'Oh, well, it's better than a master we had at my old school,' she said. 'He called me by a different name every class, and never by any chance did he hit on the right one! I believe he did it on purpose – to impress upon me that I was just one of the common herd to him. When I told him I was coming to the Wells, he sighed and said: "I thought the Wells had better taste." He was an old pig!'

'Well, he's going to be proved wrong!' exclaimed another girl, dark this time, with hazel eyes and dimples. I gathered her name was Linda. 'I think you're quite the best in our class, and I have an idea Willan thinks so, too. You've got style!'

'Thanks,' said Fizzle, making a curtsy. 'I really think we ought to go and do something. The office door has opened, and Miss Willan is due to emerge any minute.'

All day long, between lessons, we heard the film people ranging round the studios. In the distance – well in the distance – we heard Gilbert's ominously quiet and sarcastic voice making acid comments upon the film industry in general 'like flashes of lightning before the storm,' as June Two said, 'with a crack or two of thunder thrown in as a makeweight! Poor old Gilbert!'

After school we had our Character class, and, to our joy, we found the film people already in the studio waiting for us. Gilbert shot out, looking as if he'd been pulled through a hedge backwards. His hair was on end, his eyes wild, his face beaded with moisture. I expect he was glad it was Serge's turn at last!

And now came the strange part of the whole business. We had already had a ballet class during the morning to replace the one we'd missed earlier on, and I had found how very far I was behind my schoolmates. It wasn't so much that I was below standard, but that I hadn't the 'finish' of even the least advanced of them. Yet now, in this Character class, the cameramen gravitated towards me. Wherever I was, there they were, taking shots. Close-ups, too! I'm sure they imagined I was the star pupil of the class! It must have been frightfully annoying for the rest of them.

'I can't imagine what the film men thought they were doing!' exclaimed June Two, adding candidly: 'After all, you *aren't* terribly good, you know, New Girl – though, of course you may improve. Serge didn't seem to mind, either. I thought he'd have taken a fit, the way those cameramen kept pushing you in front of Fizzle, and taking umpteen shots of you doing those mazurka steps, but you'd almost think he was nodding approval! You certainly put a spell both on the cameramen and old Serge!'

'I'm awfully sorry,' I said apologetically. 'I didn't mean to get into the limelight like that, of course – being new, and everything. But I just couldn't help it, could I?'

'No, I suppose not,' admitted June. 'Anyway, you needn't apologize. We'd all have done the same if we'd had the chance! You've got to shove in the ballet if you want to get anywhere!'

After the Character class I went home by Tube, feeling that I had at least made a good beginning at the Wells. Alas! I was to learn that being good at Character, though of course it was better than nothing, didn't really get you far at the school. Sound ballet technique was its aim, and, as technique wasn't my strong point, I started at the back of the ballet class, and stayed there. Fortunately, I didn't really understand this at the time.

'Oh, I had a *thrilling* day!' I told Mariella, when she asked politely how I'd got on. 'It was wonderful having shots taken like that, and being in a film my very first day. I wonder when it will be shown – the film, I mean? They said it would be at the News Cinema.'

'Oh, it'll be years and years,' Mariella said cheerfully.

'Then they'll probably decide they won't show it after all. I know these films! They've taken two at my dancing school, and I was in one of them. I fell over doing a *pirouette*. They put that in too – called it comic relief! "Even *ballerinas* can fall down!" they said. Fancy calling *me* a *ballerina*! Fancy calling *anyone* at a dancing school a *ballerina*! Mummy was furious, and so was Madame! Oh, come on, Caroline – let's go into the park and get some fresh air. I feel stifled in here.'

140*a* Fortnum Mansions overlooked Regents Park, so we only had to go across the road to reach green grass and trees. Personally, I didn't consider that Mariella had much to grumble about.

'Yes, but I don't call this *real* grass,' she said, kicking at it with the heel of her sandal. 'All cut short with a motor lawn-mower. I like grass nibbled by sheep.'

'Oh, Mariella, you are funny!' I exclaimed. 'What a pity you don't live at Monks Hollow, your Cousin Jane's home. And the queer thing is, I don't believe *she* likes living there a bit. They're such "horsy" people, her parents, and poor Jane's scared to death of riding. You should see her at gymkhanas and things! Her face goes all white and strained. I feel very sorry for her. You see, her mother obviously expects her to do well, and poor Jane always comes in last – when she comes in at all!'

'You needn't tell me. I know!' said Mariella. 'You forget I stayed there last summer.'

'It's a pity you can't change over, isn't it?' I said. 'I believe Jane would love it here – all the dancing schools, and the theatres.'

'Yes, I've thought that, too,' said Mariella. 'But of course it's impossible. You can't argue with grown-ups. They never see the most obvious thing! Still – it's worth thinking about. You never know—'

What you never knew remained a secret. Mariella saw a policeman on horseback, and was off like the wind to watch him controlling the traffic. Even a policeman was better than nothing, Mariella said, and as a matter of fact that policeman was a jolly good rider.

When we got back to the flat, Mariella ordered Angels on Horseback for supper, because, as she said, they *sounded* equestrian, even if they *were* only winkles on toast!

Summer

Chapter I

Mariella and I Go Out Riding

THE weather began to get hot about Easter, and after I had come back to London after the holidays, Mariella suddenly announced that she was having a day off. We were on our way to her Saturday afternoon dancing class at the time – I usually went with her as far as the door. I was a little surprised, but Mariella explained in her usual headlong fashion.

'Now don't start saying "Mariella! You *told* Miss Linton—" I know I did, but after all, why should I have a beastly dancing class on Saturdays, as well as every other day of the week? *You* don't.'

'But Mariella—' I put in. 'I thought you were going to it now. I thought—'

'Well, you thought wrong,' said Mariella. 'I knew if I told you before we came out, you'd "refuse", or "run out", as Jane's cousin, Nigel, would put it, so that's why I let you think we were going dancing, when really we're going riding.'

'Riding?' I exclaimed. 'But where?'

'Oh, not in the Row, or anywhere posh,' said Mariella, 'so you needn't say: "Oh, Mariella, we're not dressed for riding!" or anything like that. I've got some jodhs for both of us in my case. You thought it was full of dismal things like point shoes and tights, didn't you?' Mariella giggled naughtily.

'I still don't think—' I began, but Mariella seized my arm.

'Here's our bus!' she exclaimed. 'So come on, Caroline – unless you want me to go by myself.'

We boarded the bus, which said 'Blackheath', so I had a vague idea that we were going south-east. Mariella climbed up top and flopped down on a seat in the front.

'As a matter of fact, it's not quite as bad as you think,' she told me. 'There wasn't a class today at all, only I knew if I said so, Honoria would have suggested something awful to take its place. A mouldy art gallery, or the Victoria and Albert, or something improving. She's full of gloomy ideas, is Honoria!'

'I think the Victoria and Albert is rather fascinating,' I answered. 'But why couldn't you have told her the truth, Mariella?'

'What? And have poor dear Honoria tramping along with us, and sighing all the time? Besides, she'd have told Mummy, most likely, and Mummy would have said no, I would break something, or sprain something, and then Honoria would have felt bound to forbid me to go. After all, Caroline, why should I not be able to do any of the things I want to do just because Mummy is a dancer, and wants *me* to be one too? It's not as if the things I want to do are wicked. Honestly, if I hadn't done something mildly exciting today I'd have bust! You don't know what a filthy temper Maestro's been in all the week. Of course, I realize now that his leg's been hurting him, and that's why he's gone to see the specialist today. But it's no use – everyone knows he'll never dance again. It's an awful tragedy really. Poor Maestro!'

As usual, Mariella had managed to turn the conversation away from her own misdemeanours.

'I didn't know your Maestro was a dancer,' I said, as the bus stopped at the traffic lights.

'Oh, yes – he was a wonderful dancer, but he had an accident, you see. It was quite recently; only last year, in fact, and he was dancing with Mummy at Covent Garden at the time. He tore some ligaments or something. If he'd been just an ordinary person, it wouldn't have been so awful, but for a male dancer – well, he's never been able to dance since.'

'Oh, I see,' I said. 'I always thought he'd been at the Wakulski-Viret School since the Year One, and that he was as old as Methuselah, with a long beard!'

Mariella burst out lauughing.

'Gosh! Maestro with a beard! I must tell the class that one! No, Maestro's quite young – just thirty-four, and he's only been at Madame's since last year. Madame held out the helping hand when he was hurt, like the angel she is. I don't suppose she ever thought of the results of her kind action, but it's a fact – loads of important people – dancers, I mean – have started coming to the studio just to learn from Maestro. Some of them are very funny. Last week a Mademoiselle Yvonne Richfaucauld, from the Paris Ballet, turned up for some private lessons. There's a crack in the panels of the studio door, and some of the boys have enlarged it, so we all took turns at having a squint at her. Well, she was warming up on the centre *barre* when I took my peep. Maestro strode in just then, and there he stood looking at her for ages, not saying anything at all. You know his way! Oh, but of course you've never seen Maestro. I keep forgetting! It's a little way he has. I expect he thinks it cows people! Well, suddenly he threw his stick across the room, and fairly yelled:

'"Mademoiselle! Cease this acrobatism at once!"

'Naturally,' added Mariella. 'She was putting across some acrobatics. They all do in the Paris Ballet. Well, then Maestro really let loose. He told her her shoulders were strained, that she waddled like a duck, that – in short, he was as rude as only Maestro can be! He finished off by exploding: "Why you to me come? I you teach cannot."'

'It sounds rather like our Classical Mime class!' I giggled. 'The *Swan Lake* bit where Odette tells the Prince she's enchanted . . . "I you greet" (makes bow) "When one me loves (hand on heart), saves, marries (points to ring), I enchanted shall be no longer.' . . . And what happened after, Mariella?'

'Oh, then he began to imitate her, and really when Maestro imitates, you can't help laughing. But Yvonne didn't. Being French, and temperamental, she burst into tears.'

'And then?' I prompted.

'Oh, then Maestro burst into tears as well,' said Mariella casually. 'He's Russian, and temperamental, too. After which they became great friends. I believe he likes her dancing very much really. He always flies out at people he likes. Gosh! Hasn't the time flown! It does when you've got someone to talk to. This is our stop. Come on, Caroline!'

As Mariella had said, the Linden Tree Riding School, Blackheath, wasn't at all a posh riding school. In fact, one might almost have called it ramshackle. There was a tangle of long grass bordering the approaches to it, and the broken-down fences were festooned with dusty bramble bushes. When we got some way down the overgrown drive, we saw that the riding school occupied the grounds of a derelict house, whose curtainless windows, with their cracked window-panes, looked back at us pathetically through the dusty summer sunshine, rather like a down-at-heel slattern who had seen better days. The various rooms of the building appeared to be used as offices and warehouses. In front of the house was an oval gravel track, with jumps (painted white) at regular intervals. On one side of the track was a row of looseboxes – obviously the old stables belonging to the mansion.

Today the gravel oval and the unkempt grass round the looseboxes was full of horses and riders. Evidently Saturday afternoon was the school's most popular day.

Mariella hailed several friends, and then after we had changed into riding clothes made straight for an end loosebox which she opened. Presently she led out a small brown pony. I couldn't help thinking she seemed pretty familiar with the place, and I wondered how many times she'd come here when she was supposed to be at her dancing school.

'Oh, hullo, Toni!' she yelled, as a young man rode past.

'Caroline, this is Toni Rossini. He's a dancer, too. He used to go to the Wells School. He's a choreographer – makes up ballets, you know. He's going to be famous. I'm sure of it! And so, incidentally, is Daddy.'

Poor Toni blushed. He seemed a very quiet, modest young man, I thought.

'Alas, no Mariella. I do not think that I shall become famous,' he said with a slightly foreign accent. 'My ballets are not really so very good, you know. But perhaps one day—'

'Don't be so modest!' exclaimed Mariella, leading out the brown pony, and brushing him down very professionally with a wisp of straw, though he was gleaming like satin already. 'Have you been doing anything in the choreographing line lately?'

'Well, yes – I do a ballet for my little friend, Veronica Weston,' said Toni. 'I call it *The Ice Maiden*. I think that it, perhaps, will be good. It is easy to compose for Veronica. She inspires one. By the way, Mariella, your friend – does she not ride?'

Mariella, who had swung herself into the saddle, dismounted again very quickly.

'Oh, Caroline – how dreadful of me!' she exclaimed. 'I'd completely forgotten about you – for the moment, I mean. But I *did* ring them up and book a mount for you. His name is King Cole, and he's over there.' She motioned with her crop (which, incidentally, she had taken from her dancing case) towards a loosebox at the far end of the row. 'I'm so sorry! Oh, and wait a minute! Here's somebody else I must introduce. Caroline, this is Josef Linsk. I expect you've heard of him. If you haven't, he'll very soon remedy that omission.' From the tone of her voice I gathered that Josef Linsk wasn't exactly a friend of Mariella's! Still, I was glad to see him. I'd heard of him so often at the Wells, and there was a lot of argument as to whether he was conceited or not. He was certainly handsome, I decided, taking in at a glance his immaculate snuff-coloured riding-breeches, that looked as if they had grown on him, and his cream silk shirt and beautifully-cut check jacket. I thought he was the best-dressed young man I had ever seen, as well as being the best-looking.

Evidently Mariella read my thoughts, for she broke in, not very politely I'm afraid:

'I didn't know you frequented this low district, Josef? I should have thought riding in the Row more in your line. More people to see you, for one thing! Also the horses here aren't quite so well behaved as the ones at your end of the town. You might fall off, you know, and damage your beautiful breeches!'

The young man's dark eyes snapped.

'Speak for yourself, my wicked one!' he retorted, and I noticed that he, too, had a slight foreign accent. 'What are these tales I heard about a young lady who precipitates herself into a bramble bush not so very long ago! It was that especial bramble bush, I think.' He pointed with his crop at an especially dusty clump of prickly vegetation on the edge of an overgrown copse.

'Oh, *that*!' Mariella had the grace to blush. 'Someone dashed out behind me, and Kitty shied. I was up in a trice.' Then she added wickedly: 'Josef, you know, used to go to my dancing school, but that was long before my time. He's ever so old, really.'

'Twenty-four,' said the young man, balancing easily in the saddle, while his mount danced and pawed the ground, impatient to be off.

'Oh, is that all? Well, you *look* much older,' declared Mariella. 'Hadn't you better saddle up King Cole, Caroline. I'm just off over the jumps. I'll come back for you in a jiffy. Goodbye!'

She was away towards the track, her slender graceful figure looking its best on horseback. The sun glinted in her red-gold mop of curls, making it look like a halo, and her green eyes were fairly snapping with excitement. She sailed over the jumps in fine style. There was no doubt about it – she was certainly a very good rider.

'Have you ridden long?' I asked her when she came back to me. 'You seem awfully good. Did you learn here?'

'Oh, no,' she said. 'Didn't I tell you? Jane's cousin, Nigel, taught me when I was staying at Monks Hollow last summer.' Then she added in her usual frank fashion: 'Yes, I do *ride* rather well, don't I?'

We spent a lovely afternoon at the riding school, which was really very nice, in spite of its unprepossessing appearance. One of the rooms of the house had been turned into a small café where pupils could get tea. Someone living on the premises made the cakes, and I had to agree with Mariella that they beat the ones we got at the flat hollow.

'Nothing like home-made things,' she declared, beginning on the third piece of sandwich cake. 'Although they may not *look* so wonderful, they don't at least taste all the same!'

After tea we took the ponies away from the school, and out on to a bit of open country near.

'There's only one thing I'm worried about, Mariella,' I said, as we cantered along, side by side. 'Isn't this most frightfully expensive?'

'Oh, so-so,' Mariella said offhandedly. 'But Daddy has loads of money, so why worry!' Then, seeing my puzzled expression, she went on: 'Oh, don't look so careworn, Caroline. It's not really as bad as you think. You see, Daddy knows all about the riding school. At least, I told him I wanted a cheque for my riding lesson, so it's his own fault if he didn't actually take it in. Anyway, he took his head out of a glass case where he'd been arranging something and murmured: "Ming, 9th Dynasty", and wrote me the cheque like the lamb he is. I have an idea he *did* know, as a matter of fact.' She sighed, and stroked her pony's tawny neck. 'I have an idea Daddy realizes I shall never be a dancer – not a wonderful one, like Mummy. You see, Daddy, being a critic, knows in a minute if you'll ever be any good. As a matter of fact, I think Mummy knows it, too, only she's like an ostrich.'

'An ostrich?' I gasped.

'Yes – head in the sand, you know,' explained Mariella. 'She just can't face the fact that her own daughter isn't going to follow in her footsteps – I should say ballet shoes, shouldn't I! Oh, well – let's forget the gloomy future! Let's live for the day! Let's gallop like mad! Come on, Caroline! Let's pretend this place is near Monks Hollow. Race you to the cairn!'

The 'cairn' was a tumbledown heap of stones that had obviously been a blitzed house. Incidentally, it was rather pretty now, completely covered as it was with purple willow-herb.

We got home about six o'clock, and Mariella told Miss Linton she'd had a beastly class. 'Maestro was in a filthy temper,' she added.

When we were in bed that night a whisper from the next bed – I shared Mariella's room – showed that Mariella's conscience was troubling her.

'It's not that I'm deceitful, really, Caroline,' she said, and you could hear the sound of tears in her voice. 'It's just that I love riding so much. You don't know how I long to be outside doing *real* things. I hate spending my time trying to make my legs turn the way they were never meant to! I hate not having to lift things in case I get musclely arms! I hate not being able to eat all the *nice* things – like ices, and cream buns – in case I get fat! I *want* musclely arms!' cried Mariella, lifting both soft white arms above her head, and looking at them in disgust. 'I *want* to heave things! Gosh! Why did I happen to be born the daughter of a *prima ballerina*!'

There was silence for a bit, then Mariella began to giggle.

'Caroline – are you awake?'

'W-what's the matter?' I grunted sleepily.

'It's just that I wanted to ask you to remind me to take my riding things out of my case tomorrow before I go to class. You see, it's my dancing case, and I can imagine the stir it would cause if I turned up for a ballet class with jodhpurs instead of tights, and a hoof-pick instead of ballet shoes!'

Chapter 2

I Receive a Letter and Write One

THE next morning I got a letter from Mummy.

My darling Caroline,

We were so glad to have your letter with all the news about London and your school, and your little friend, Mariella. Here things have gone on much as usual, and very little has happened since you went back after the Easter holidays. The weather has been very cold here as it usually is in spring, and there is still snow on Corbie's Nob, and on Ravens' Eyrie. There are lambs in the South Meadow, and they seem to be doing well, in spite of the cold. Those down at Hordon are quite big, but of course everything is a month earlier, at least, down there.

The daffodils are lovely round the lake. Fiona picked a lot last weekend when she was home for half-term. Ian Frazer came over from Lingfield and helped her to pick them. They took them to a Newcastle wholesaler in Ian's car, and sold them for six pounds. Fiona bought herself some nylons with the money. Poor Fiona! I'm afraid she minds being poor a lot – more than you do, Caroline.

There were the usual Horse Sports at Dewburn last Saturday. I enclose an account which came out in the Hexham paper. You'll find a lot of names you know in it.

'I think I've told you all the news. Oh, no – one more thing. Your Uncle Adrian had dinner with us last night, and he says Sebastian has won an Exhibition, and has gone abroad to study, so I'm afraid you won't be able to see him in London for a bit.

With love from us all,

MUMMY

PS – Are you happy at the Wells?

A few days later I wrote back to Mummy, and this is what I said:

140*a* Fortnum Mansions,
London, W1.

Darling Mummy,

Thank you awfully for your letter. It seems queer to hear about snow on Corbie's Nob. Here, it is getting quite hot; at least it feels hot to me, though Mariella says it's only lukewarm! London looks very nice, just now; the trees in Leicester Square are lovely. They haven't had time to get dusty yet!

It was nice of you to remember to cut out the bit in the paper about the Horse Sports at Dewburn, and send it to me. I can just imagine you all there – you and Daddy in the car, and Uncle Adrian on his bicycle, and Fiona and Ian in Ian's car. I wonder why Ian wasn't riding in the sports? He usually does. He usually wins, too, because – no, I'd better not say why he wins, as he seems to be a special friend of Fiona's!

Reading the Hexham paper made me feel quite homesick. I kept thinking of all the people I know riding over to the Sports on their ponies. It made me want to be there, too! I see that Guy Charlton, who lives at Hordon Castle, won the Over 16, Under 18, Mile Over Fences, and David Eliot won the VC Race, and the Musical Ride.

Oh, yes – I am ever so happy at the Wells. The Character classes are lovely. I get quite a lot of attention from Serge. I think he really likes me. He calls me by my name, anyway, though he does pronounce it 'Carol-een'. Mostly he just calls people 'you'!

I love staying with Mariella. Uncle Oscar is very kind when he remembers you're there, and so is Aunt Irma whenever we see her. That isn't very often because she's usually at the theatre, or travelling round with the Company. Aunt Irma is beautiful to look at – 'petite', I think they call it, with a pale oval face and the hugest velvety

We saw Antonio and Rosario

dark eyes you ever saw. When I first came to the Mansions, I kept on wondering who it was she reminded me of. Mariella said: 'Oh, it's my cousin, Jane Foster. She's the very image of Mummy.' And it's quite true – she is!

Talking of Jane reminds me that Mariella said when I wrote home would I ask you to give Jane her love. And you know Nigel Monkhouse, Jane's cousin – he's that fair, good-looking boy who always wins a lot of things in gymkhanas? Well, Mariella says would you give him a message from her. Just say: 'Jolly good!' and he'll understand. I think she's referring to the Pony Sports at Dewburn where he won the Under 16 Jumping.

There's no one very interesting in London just now – interesting to me, I mean. Veronica is touring with the Second Company. Someone did tell me she's going into the First Company soon, but I don't know if it's true. Sebastian, as you said in your letter, is abroad too, and his friend, Angelo, is in Spain, studying Spanish, music, and dancing. Mariella and I went to the Spanish Ballet at the Stoll Theatre a week or so ago. We saw Antonio and Rosario. They were *wonderful*! I think I liked Rosario best – she's so lovely to look at, besides being so good a dancer, but of course, Antonio's footwork is wonderful. You should see his *Zapateado* and his *Bolero*! I wish we did more Spanish dancing at the Wells, but of course we only touch on it in the Character classes. I wish we played castanets in the Character classes. They would certainly liven them up a bit! But as someone said jokingly the other day when I suggested it in the dressing-room: 'No castanets at the Wells, my dear, not in the regular curriculum! They never played the castanets at the Russian Imperial School, so of course we can't play them here!'

This is a very long letter, so I expect a nice long one in reply.

Lots of love,

CAROLINE

The Third Year

Winter

Chapter I

We See Piccadilly Circus By Night

WINTER in London was very different from winter in Northumberland. Instead of frosted trees and sparkling snowdrifts, fogs hung over the city, so that you never saw even a glimpse of sunshine. I think that by the time the fog lifted – if it ever really did lift during those gloomy days – the sun had already set. It was a dark winter, everyone said, and perhaps that was why I noticed the difference between 140*a* Fortnum Mansions and my own lovely home in the far-off north of England. During these cheerless days I longed for the sight of a dancing log fire, or glimpse of the sunset glow turning to soft pink the shattered peak of Ravens' Eyrie. Several times I dreamt I was climbing through the bracken to Corbie's Nob, where I could look down upon the wintry Border country, and see Cheviot's round brow, capped with snow, away to the north-east. When Mummy wrote and said they'd been skating on the lake, I longed to have a magic carpet to take me there in the twinkling of an eye, and drop me down in the semicircle of silver sand by the boathouse. In my imagination I could hear Sebastian calling for me: 'Hey, Caroline! Coming for a ride?' Or Trixie's soft Northumbrian burr: 'Come you in, Miss Caroline! It's time for your supper. There's freshly baked bread, and a singing-hinny, fairly running with butter, just the way you like it.'

Mariella was very busy these days. She hadn't even time for her riding school. She was taking her Intermediate RAD exam, and she seemed to think it was touch-and-go whether she would get it or not.

'And I simply *must* get it,' she confided in me, 'because, you see, poor Mummy's head would be bowed with shame if her – Irma Foster's – daughter were to fail an ordinary common or garden RAD exam.'

Poor Mariella! I did pity her! It seemed awful to have to do a thing you loathed just because you happened to have a mother who did it superlatively well.

One night we slipped out of the flat and took a bus to Piccadilly Circus to see the lights, although we weren't supposed to be out alone at night.

It was fun standing underneath the Eros statue, and dodging the spurts of water blown from the dolphins' mouths by the light wind. The shallow steps glimmered icily, and reflected the colours of the huge lighted signs round the Circus.

'I think Bovril is the most thrilling one,' I said. 'The fountain, or whatever it is, especially.'

'Oh, no – I like the Guinness clock,' said Mariella.

'Look out!' I warned. 'It's an awfully wet spot just here. Your stockings are absolutely soaked, Mariella!'

'What do I care!' shrieked Mariella excitedly. 'I can change them when I get home, can't I? Look at all these people dressed in funny clothes! Oh, I think they're collecting for something – they're rattling boxes.'

Suddenly, while we watched, two figures emerged from the group – a slim, dark young man, and a dark-haired girl. They faced each other, fingers pointed, and then began to dance, castanets clicking, feet stamping.

'Angelo!' I shrieked. 'Oh, Angelo – it's *me*, Caroline!'

When he saw me his face lit up, and his dark eyes sparkled.

'Oh, it is you, Caroline! What are you doing here? I did not know you were in London.'

'I live here now,' I answered. 'Hasn't Sebastian told you? I'm learning dancing.'

'Dancing?' Angelo repeated. 'You mean—' He struck an attitude and tapped out a few steps with his feet, his castanets clicking.

'Oh, no!' I laughed. 'Not *that* sort of dancing. I'm at the Wells. There aren't any castanets at the Wells. It's mostly classical ballet.'

'Ah! classical ballet. That is cold, alas!' said Angelo with a shiver. 'It reminds me that winter is already here. Oh, for the warm sun of Spain!'

'That reminds me,' I said. 'I thought you were in Spain. Mummy said you were studying there.'

'During the summer vacation, yes,' said Angelo. 'But in October I come back here. I hope to return later. At the present I am moving round from place to place – anywhere where I can dance. Tomorrow it will be Blackpool.'

'Then you've decided not to go to the University to study,' I said.

Angelo shrugged his shoulders expressively.

'That has been decided for me – for the present, at any rate. There is no room for me. I must wait. Sometimes I think that the life of a university is not for me. I must dance—'

'By the way, this is Mariella,' I said, drawing her forward. 'I live in her flat, and we're not supposed to be out here at night, so I think we ought to go. Goodbye, Angelo!'

'*Adios, señorita!*' he replied.

The dark girl plucked him by the arm.

'Yes, come along, Angelo! Are you going to stand there talking all night!' It was obvious from her voice that she was English, and also, I thought, a little cross.

'Very well, Margarita – I come,' Angelo answered with another shrug.

In a moment they were gone, swallowed up by the crowd, and all we could hear were Spanish cries and stamping feet.

'Have you any money, Mariella?' I said, as the rattle of

collecting boxes reached us. 'I've only got sixpence.'

'I've got one, too,' Mariella said. 'What are you collecting for anyway?' she asked the young man who tendered the box. 'I always like to know what I'm giving money to.'

The young man smiled at her grown-up manner.

'Oh, it's a good cause – one you'll approve of,' he assured her with a grin. 'It's the Dumb Animals Defence Association, and this particular collection is going to the Welfare of Old and Worn Out Carthorses section.'

'Oh, if it's anything to do with horses, I think I might find you a shilling,' Mariella said grandly, rummaging in her pocket. 'I hope you make good use of the money you collect.'

'It's all used for the good of the cause, lady,' said the young man, grinning broadly. I have an idea he was an art student, judging by his flowing tie and broad-brimmed hat. 'No expensive salaries, I assure you. Everything on a voluntary basis. Take those two dancers. They've given their services for nothing. Made a deal of money.'

Then he was gone, too, rattling his box as he went. A policeman grinned indulgently as he dodged through the traffic to rejoin his companions on the far side of the Circus.

I felt very lonely after they had gone. Angelo had seemed like an old friend. But I wasn't lonely for long. Another crowd of people was surging round the steps.

'Football fans!' Mariella said knowledgeably. 'There must have been a big match on.'

Then, suddenly, it seemed to me that I was back in my own home town. The newcomers were obviously strangers to London, and were seeing the sights. They were pointing out the lighted signs, and the language they were doing it in was – Tyneside!

'By, lad! That's a good 'un! It is, an' aal!' exclaimed a man wearing a toy sailor hat stuck on the back of his head. 'It's a proper bit of all reet!'

'Get away, man! It's not as good as this'n!' said another, pointing out the Bovril sign.

'Aye! It's got wor toon beat to a frazzle. It has, an' aal!' said a third. 'There's enough light here to light up aal the bits of villages in Northumberland wot's still got paraffin lamps and candles!' said a fourth.

They stood for a moment under the shadow of Eros, lost in silent admiration. Then they, too, were gone; and Mariella and I stood alone once more.

'Oh, Mariella – let's go,' I said, blinking away a tear that would persist in trickling down my nose.

'What's the matter?' asked Mariella. 'Why, you're crying, Caroline!'

'It's nothing, really,' I said. 'It was just hearing those people. It made me so dreadfully homesick. It was like being back in my own home – like walking up Northumberland Street on a Saturday night!'

Mariella said nothing, but she tucked her arm through mine in a way that made me feel she sympathized, even if she didn't understand. Somehow I couldn't imagine Mariella feeling homesick. She wasn't fond enough of her home for that!

Chapter 2

Mostly about a Phone Call

THE winter term dragged on, and sometimes I felt that it would never end. Then, all at once, it was the week before Christmas, and in two days' time I was due to go home for the holidays. I felt like cheering! I got a letter that morning from Mummy. It was a short one, she said, because Fiona was home from school, and Dolly, the girl who helped Trixie with the cooking, now that we hadn't a cook any longer, had got tonsillitis. She added that, with Christmas only a week away, she was running round in circles! Enclosed with the letter (which was registered) were five one-pound notes for my return ticket and a sleeper. She said I had better come third class, this time, as we had simply got to economize.

'How awful!' exclaimed Mariella. 'You won't sleep a wink, Caroline. Why, there are several people all together in the third class!'

'Four berths,' I said with a smile. 'Don't worry, Mariella. I shan't sleep a wink, anyhow. I'm far too excited. I don't care if I have to sit on the running-board, or perch on the cow-catcher all the way to Newcastle, as long as I get there in the end! As a matter of fact, I think it'll be rather fun having other people with me in the compartment. They'll be ever such nice people, most likely.'

'I expect they'll be *awful* people,' said Mariella. 'Horrible women with pince-nez and woollen combinations! Tell you what, Caroline – I'll get a cheque from Daddy, and then you can go first class.'

'Well, I shan't worry about their combinations!' I laughed. 'You are funny, Mariella! And of course I couldn't dream of letting you ask Uncle Oscar for a cheque, though it's awfully sweet of you to think of it.'

'Oh, well – it's your funeral,' Mariella said huffily. I think she didn't like the idea of my going away, and of course I can see it would be very dull for her, being by herself. 'When do you go?'

'Tomorrow night,' I said, turning *déboulées* round the bedroom, to the imminent danger of Mariella's collection of china horses. 'Oh, Mariella, I'm so *thrilled*!'

'Well, you needn't show it!' grumbled Mariella. 'Of course I know you hate being here—'

'Of *course* I don't hate being here,' I burst out, stopping in the middle of a turn. 'You *couldn't* think I hated being here, Mariella! But, after all, Bracken Hall is my *home*.'

'Oh, yes, I know. It's just – well, I shall miss you most awfully, Caroline. I do wish you were spending Christmas here.'

I put both my arms round her.

'Oh, don't look so sad, Mariella. Next holidays you must come and stay with me. Mummy will love to have you.'

'I'd adore to,' Mariella said fervently. 'But I don't think Mummy would let me.'

'Why ever not?' I demanded.

'Well, you see, my audition for the Wells is at the end of the summer hols, so I'm supposed to practise night and day.' She sighed deeply. 'Perhaps if I fail to get in, Mummy will realize I'm no good, and then perhaps she'll let me come and stay with you... Oh, there's the telephone! I'd better go. It'll be for Daddy, and I can say he's out more convincingly than you, Caroline. You've got such an awkward conscience!'

She dashed out of the room, and into the tiny square hall, out of which all the rooms in No 140*a* opened. In a second or two she was back.

'Caroline! Come quickly! It's a long-distance call for you. It's from Northumberland, and I think it's your mother. Be quick! There's half a minute of your three gone already!'

It's funny to think that those short two and a half minutes were enough to turn my joy to sorrow, and to shatter all the lovely castles I'd been building in the air about my forthcoming holiday. In those two and a half minutes Mummy explained that Dolly's tonsillitis wasn't tonsillitis at all, but diphtheria, and that, as she and Fiona had both been with her, and neither had had the disease, they were both in quarantine. I hadn't had it, either, so on no account was I to go home.

'It's lucky you're so happy in your London home with Mariella,' added Mummy. 'Of course we shall all miss you dreadfully, dear, but I expect you'll have a lovely time, all the same. I'll send on your presents and cards, of course.'

'Oh, yes, Mummy – thank you,' I whispered back into the telephone, trying not to let my sick disappointment sound in my voice.

'Well, goodbye, dear,' came Mummy's voice at the other end. 'It's not so very long till the Easter holidays, after all, is it? Have a good time!' The pips went, and I heard the little click as she put the receiver down. Then all those miles and miles of dark and unfriendly country rolled between us once more, cutting me off from my beloved home and all the people I ached to see.

'Well? What was it all about?' came Mariella's voice, breaking in upon my daydream.

'You've got your wish,' I said, laying down the telephone. 'I can't go home after all. Dolly's got diphtheria, not just tonsillitis, and they're all in quarantine.'

For a moment Mariella stood quite still. Then she fell upon me, and began to dance a jig.

'Oh, Caroline! How lovely! Oh, of course, I'm most frightfully sorry you can't go – sorry for *you*, that is. But we'll have a wonderful time here – really we will. Caroline – don't cry! It will be lovely – it will truly. You can teach me exactly how you do things at Christmas in Northumberland, and we'll do them here.'

I hadn't the heart to tell her that cutting down your own

Christmas tree out of your own wood; driving to parties along snowy roads in your own sleigh; going to a candlelit carol service in the village church, not to mention seeing the New Year in in the real North Country fashion, were things you couldn't possibly do in a London flat, no matter how luxurious it was, or how hard you tried, or how much money you possessed.

'We'll have a Christmas tree,' she was saying, 'and on Christmas Day we'll have our Christmas dinner downstairs in the restaurant – we always do and it will be great fun, now that you're here.'

I smiled through my tears, because it would have spoilt things for Mariella if I had gone on crying.

'Yes, I expect it'll be great fun,' I said, 'once I get used to spending Christmas away from home.'

Chapter 3

Christmas in London

IT was a gloomy business taking all the presents I had so painstakingly collected out of my suitcase, and wrapping them up to be sent off by post. Mariella insisted upon helping me, and of course she wanted to know who each one was for.

'Those are for Trixie,' I said, 'and you needn't say rude things about them, Mariella, because Trixie always wears wool-plated stockings of that peculiar shade of grey, and she wouldn't thank you for wonderful nylons, even if I could have afforded them. And that teeny-weeny flower vase is for Mummy. She can fill it with the first violets from the wood, and it will look lovely standing on top of the piano, and reflecting in the polished surface. This brooch is for Fiona. I expect she'll sniff at it because the stones aren't real, but it's awfully pretty, don't you think?'

'Yes, it is rather sweet,' agreed Mariella. 'What have you got for your father?'

'Daddy's present took an awful lot of thought,' I answered. 'What *does* one give to a "successful businessman"? – and I have an idea that he's not even very successful either, nowadays!'

'Cigars,' said Mariella promptly.

'Oh, I never thought of them,' I confessed. 'Besides, even if I had, cigars would have been far too expensive, and I couldn't very well give him *one* cigar, could I? It wouldn't seem much of a present.'

'No, I suppose it wouldn't,' agreed Mariella.

'Anyway, I've embroidered his initials on a white linen hankie,' I said. 'I think he'll like that. After all, he's got to keep blowing his nose, hasn't he, so it doesn't matter how many people give him hankies – they'll always come in useful. I think that's the lot. Oh, no – there's a present for Dolly in the very bottom of the case. It's a bottle of carnation scent. Oh, I know it's terribly strong, Mariella, but you needn't wrinkle up your nose. Dolly adores it. She told me so. Poor Dolly! I hope she isn't frightfully ill with diphtheria.'

'Oh, no – nowadays diphtheria is quite a mild disease,' Mariella said in her most grown-up manner. 'She'll be well in no time – at least,' she added rather more cautiously, 'she'll be well as soon as the holidays are over. Of course, the quarantine period's rather long, I believe.'

I couldn't help bursting into a peal of laughter, despite my fit of the blues. Mariella was very funny at times. She wasn't really very subtle!

We certainly had everything money could buy for my London Christmas as Mariella had promised. Christmas dinner in the restaurant was very festive. The big room was gay with balloons and streamers, and there was a huge Christmas tree with a present on it for each guest. There were long tables loaded with expensive crackers, each one made in the shape of a different flower, with a glittering centre. Mine was a water-lily, and Mariella's was an exotic orchid. They had wonderful gifts inside, besides paper hats and mottoes. I couldn't help thinking that Maud Frazer would have approved! My present was a tiny penknife with a mother-of-pearl handle, and Mariella's was a ballet dancer brooch.

'You see!' she said in disgust. 'I can't get away from ballet, even in a cracker!'

'All right, let's exchange,' I suggested.

'Done!' said Mariella promptly. 'I'd like the knife lots better, though I don't suppose it would really be much use to me in the hunting field.'

I couldn't help laughing, though as a matter of fact Mariella was quite serious.

After dinner was over, and Santa Claus had come and gone,

we played games, sang community songs, and danced things like The Grand Old Duke of York, and Sir Roger de Coverley, and after that, it was nine o'clock and bedtime, so we went up in the lift to the flat. While Mariella was in the bathroom, I went out on to the little balcony outside our bedroom window and leaned my arms upon the railings. The night was clear and frosty, and you could actually see the moon floating in a pale starlit sky. I wondered what they were doing in far-away Northumberland, and if they were thinking of me, as I was of them. It seemed queer to know that the same old moon was shining down serenely on all of us.

Chapter 4

Changes at Home

I THOUGHT the Easter holidays would never come, but at last they did, and this time nothing happened to stop me from boarding the northbound afternoon Pullman train, which was Mummy's compromise between first and third class. Poor Mariella was so busy with her dancing that, as she said herself, she hadn't even time to be lonely!

'Having to practise that beastly ballet day and night has its compensations,' she said philosophically. 'I shan't have time even to miss you, Caroline. Gosh! Shan't I be glad when I've had that beastly audition and been turned down flat! Then, perhaps, I shall have a little peace. Maybe I shall even be allowed a holiday at your home. Perhaps I could stay for a whole week with you, and another with my cousin, Jane. Oh, wouldn't it be heavenly! Do you think your mother would have me, Caroline?'

'Oh, I expect she'd put up with you – if it was only for a week!' I teased.

When I got home I found that things had changed a lot. Mummy looked after the house herself now, with the help of Trixie and a daily 'char' who came in from the village. Even Dolly, who had helped Trixie with the cooking, had been found another place. She'd gone to Lingfield Lodge to be the Frazers' kitchen-maid. Daddy drove himself to town in a Ford Prefect, instead of the palatial Rolls. The shooting-brake had been sold (together with the shooting on the Bracken estate), and Mummy had given up her little Austin, and now rode a bicycle or walked. As a consequence, she was a lot slimmer, and now had really a lovely figure. Perkins had got another job as chauffeur to Lady Blantosh at Blantosh Castle, and we only had one gardener – Dickson – and he had to keep an eye on my pony, Gillyflower, while I was at school, as well as looking after the gardens. Fiona had a new hunter which she kept over at Lingfield in the Frazers' stables, because she said she certainly wasn't going to muck the Bracken stable out herself, thank you! At Lingfield there was a full-time groom who did all that.

Bit by bit, the Hall gardens lost their park-like appearance. The front lawns were kept cut, and the hedges trimmed, but out of sight of the house the celandine reigned supreme; and later on in the year the daisies flourished, and the dandelions bloomed in golden splendour. I thought they looked beautiful, but Mummy sighed when she saw them. As for Fiona, she looked down her beautiful nose at them, and said in a very superior way that she didn't know what on earth people would think.

'What does it matter what they think?' I flared up. 'I suppose by "people" you mean that horrible Ian Frazer?'

'You'd better stop calling Ian names,' said Fiona coldly, 'because I'm going to marry him.'

For a few seconds I just stood there with my mouth open, too astonished to say anything.

'Fiona, you're *not*!'

'Yes, I am,' answered my sister. 'Why not, anyway? If you think I'm going to stay here all among the daisies and the dandelions, wearing the summer-before-last's dresses, having to wash up on Trixie's day out, then you're mistaken! I'm tired of having to go to town in a dirty, smelly bus along with the village people because Daddy's got the one and only car! If you think I'm going to let people call *me* "poor Fiona Scott", and say: "Of course the Scotts were well off once, but they've come down in the world, and now they're as poor as church mice, poor things!" If you think I'm going to let them say *that*, then you're mistaken again!' declared Fiona, with a toss of her golden head. '*I'll* show them, the old cats! So, if you want to know, *that's* why I'm going to marry Ian.'

'But you don't love him!' I said. 'You *couldn't* love him, Fiona! In my own opinion, nobody in their right minds could possibly love Ian Frazer, with his lying, cheating ways.

'You don't understand,' said Fiona. 'You're only a kid. Love doesn't come into it. Love is only something you read about in fairy tales. "The Prince and Princess lived happily ever after!" Nobody believes in that sort of romantic rubbish when they're grown up. I daresay I shall get along all right, and at least I shall be rich.'

'Oh, Fiona – I'm sure you're wrong!' I argued. 'I may be only a kid, but I'm sure love isn't only in fairy tales. Look at Veronica and Sebastian. I'm sure Veronica loves Sebastian—'

'Yes, look at Veronica!' scoffed Fiona. 'A fat lot of good it's done Veronica getting keen on Sebastian! Why, he's never spoken to her, or written to her since she left Bracken all that time ago. I don't believe Sebastian cares a toss for Veronica!'

'That's because you're jealous,' I flung at her. 'You always *were* jealous of Sebastian being keen on Veronica.'

'I tell you he isn't keen. If he was, why should he behave like that?' demanded Fiona.

'Because he's a musician, and temperamental. They're both temperamental,' I said, trying to explain, though I didn't really understand myself. 'It may seem queer to us, but it doesn't mean they don't love each other.'

'Oh, all right! All right!' snapped Fiona. 'Have it your own way, only leave me alone. I shall be engaged to Ian before very long – you'll see.'

'You aren't old enough,' I argued. 'You're only just eighteen. You haven't left school yet.'

'Well, lots of people are *married* at eighteen – let alone engaged,' she told me. 'People always used to get married young in the olden days. Anyway, Mummy has promised I shall leave school at the end of next term.'

I saw it wasn't the least use arguing with her, and, sure enough, a few days before I went back to London, Fiona blossomed forth in a simply enormous diamond engagement ring. Incidentally, Mummy made her promise to take it off and wear it on a ribbon round her neck when she went back to school for her last term.

I think that most people were very impressed by the size of the ring, but privately I thought it was rather vulgar, though I daren't tell Fiona so. Fiona, herself, was as proud as a peacock, and lost no opportunity of showing it off. I even caught her pouring out afternoon tea with her left hand, and turning over the pages of her prayer-book in church with one glove off, obviously entranced by the multi-coloured flashes her ring made in the sunlight shining through the stained-glass window.

Of course we had to tell Sebastian the news. I wrote a long letter to him, and Mummy addressed it to the place with the funny name where he'd gone to study music. As usual, his reply wasn't the least what you'd expect. It wasn't a letter at all, for one thing. It was merely a sheet of music paper with half a dozen lines of music written upon it. At the top was printed:

> Bridal March – especially composed for Fiona Scott, spinster, upon her marriage to Ian Frazer, gentleman (?), by the celebrated composer, Sebastian Scott. Copyright in all countries.

The treble clef was made in the shape of a caricature of Fiona, and the bass was one of Ian. Underneath was written:

> Suggested nuptual hymn for the happy couple, No 450 Ancient & Modern: *Fight the Good Fight.*

I tried to play the music on the piano in the lounge, but whether my music had gone down – it was never very good in the first place – or whether Sebastian's writing was hard to read, I don't know. Anyway, it just didn't sound like music at all. Finally, I took it down to Uncle Adrian, Sebastian's father, who plays beautifully. He played a couple of lines, and then began to laugh.

'Well, let's hope Fiona and Ian's married life won't turn out to be as discordant as this!' he said. 'I suppose the young monkey has been influenced by all this modern stuff. Or perhaps he *meant* it to be discordant!'

Oh, yes! I was quite sure Sebastian meant it all right! I decided I had better not show his effort to my sister, or she'd have her knife into Sebastian even deeper than she had at present.

It was awful how quickly the holidays slipped away. I expect it was because there was so much to do in them. The Frazers had a tennis party, and Fiona enjoyed herself immensely, queening it as an engaged girl; engaged, moreover, to the son and heir of the house. Jane Foster was there, and Nigel, her cousin, and I gave them Mariella's messages, though Mummy had already done so. I went to a dancing class at Miss Martin's, having first asked permission from the Wells before I left London. I found that Jane was quite twice as good as I was!

'Oh, Jane – I can't think how you do *pirouettes* like that!' I exclaimed. 'They're miles better than mine, though you're younger than me, and you haven't learnt nearly as long. Honestly, I don't believe Mariella's are as good as yours are.'

Jane blushed. She was very modest.

'Oh, Caroline – do you really think so?' she said.

'I don't *think* – I know!' I insisted. 'Miss Martin knows, too. You can tell by the way she smiles when you do them. You've got a wonderful style, you know, Jane. I can tell that with being at the Wells.'

Yes, Miss Martin obviously thought the world of Jane, whereas she was just as obviously disappointed in me, though she tried hard not to show it. The only thing she was enthusiastic about was my Character, and she made me do a Hungarian peasant dance before the whole class, to show them how it ought to be done, and on another day I showed them a Jota – a Spanish gipsy dance.

I went to a dancing class at Miss Martin's

'What a funny name!' exclaimed Jane after I'd finished. 'How do you spell it?'

'J-O-T-A,' I answered. 'But it's pronounced "Ho-ta".'

'You do it beautifully, Caroline. I could watch you for ever!' said Jane dreamily – she was a very dreamy girl. 'It makes me think of hot, sunny Spain, and oranges, and white stockings, and bougainvilia, and *patias*, and romantic Spanish lovers serenading their lady-loves under a white Spanish moon.'

I couldn't help laughing – she sounded so serious.

But it was true. Character was the only thing I was good at. I couldn't even deceive myself any more – I wasn't really making any progress at the Wells. In fact, sometimes I thought I'd gone down after leaving Miss Martin's, and I believe she thought so, too.

It was awful having to answer people's questions as to how I was getting on at the Wells. I tried hard to smile cheerfully and answer: 'Oh, I'm getting on frightfully well, Mrs Robertson, thank you. Yes, I love being in London – the Wells is fine. Do you want to speak to Mummy? I think she's just coming.' Then I'd escape as quickly as possible, and run upstairs to the attics when I'd practise *pirouettes* and *entrechats*, trying to do them like Jane, though I knew I never would. Afterwards I would creep sadly down to the stables, and lay my head on Gillyflower's warm, silky neck, and wish I had never learned to dance at all.

Summer

Chapter 1

Dark Days

AND now began the darkest period of my life. Not that anyone was unkind to me at the Wells. On the contrary, they were all sweet. The fault – if you can call it that – lay in my dancing. I felt all the time as if I were struggling against fearful odds – as if I just couldn't make the grade. For one thing, I couldn't get the necessary 'turned-out' line, and when I forced my limbs into this position, my shoulders became strained, and my expression harassed; for another, something about the dancing, itself, didn't seem to appeal to me. I wanted to dance – of that I was still quite sure – but not *this* sort of dancing. Not this endless repetition of *pirouettes*, *développés*, *battements*. Day in, day out, it seemed to be a never-ending routine of impossibly difficult steps, with never a real, lively dance to relieve the monotony. Frankly I was bored. When we did the graceful *ports de bras*, I longed to throw up my arms and shout – *anything* to wake them up! I couldn't help thinking what a sensation it would have caused in the stately ballet class if I *had* given one really good, wild, war-whoop – like Angelo did when he danced! But even in the Character class no one gave war-whoops – not even genteel ones. Yet it was only in the Character classes that I was really happy.

'You know you're really awfully good at Character,' said Marion, who was in my form, and who couldn't do Character for toffee, and knew it. 'Gosh! I believe you're Serge's favourite pupil.' She flopped down on a bench near the dressing-room door, and fanned herself vigorously with somebody's tights. 'He got quite excited when you did that Spanish thing today – more excited than I've ever seen the old boy! Funny if you turned out to be a Margot Fonteyn in reverse!'

'Whatever do you mean?' I demanded.

'Oh, you know the story,' put in June Two. 'Fonteyn came to the Wells with a reputation for Character, and left it as the world's greatest classical dancer.'

'Well, I don't think I'm likely to be the world's greatest anything,' I said gloomily. 'Apart from Serge's classes, which are fun, I'm the world's worst.'

'Yes, you certainly aren't the world's best when it comes to classical ballet,' declared June candidly. 'You just don't seem to get on any further. If you don't mind my asking, Caroline, what made you come to the Wells in the first place? Were you sent by doting parents, or what?'

'Oh, *no*!' I said. 'Mummy doesn't really agree with ballet. She has the old-fashioned idea about the stage. I came here because I wanted to dance, only now I'm here I just don't seem to be any good at it.'

'Oh, well, cheer up!' Marion said bracingly. 'We can't all be *prima ballerinas*, can we? And Serge seems to like you.'

'Yes, wasn't that Sevillanas lovely?' I said, cheering up a bit at the thought of it. 'It made me think of Angelo—'

'Angelo? Sounds familiar. Boyfriend of yours?'

'Oh, no!' I laughed. 'He's just someone I know slightly. His name is Angelo Ibañez.'

'Ah! That rings a bell!' said Marion. 'He dances, doesn't he? Spanish, or something. I've heard he's rather wonderful.'

'Fancy you knowing Angelo!' I exclaimed. 'Or rather knowing *about* him. Yes, he's a Spanish dancer, and he used to stay with a cousin of mine at my home. Well, one Christmas – not last Christmas, because I had to stay in London then; Dolly, one of our maids got diphtheria; but the Christmas before – we went to a party, and Angelo danced. He taught me some of the steps—' I stood up and demonstrated, and very soon the whole room was watching, several girls from the Senior School, as well as the Juniors.

'Oh, lovely, Caroline! Serge should have been here to see!' said Barbara, another friend of mine. Incidentally, she was an American girl and had an accent you could cut with a knife. 'He'd sure have fallen on your neck and wept! You've got everything it takes, honey, when it comes to Character, and that's a fact! You've got the fire, the flash of the eye, the pep, the – abandon, I think is the word.'

For a time I felt happier. It was nice to think there was *something* in the dancing line I could do, even if it wasn't actual ballet. But it didn't last for long. After all, Character dancing isn't taken very seriously at the Wells where the accent is all on the pure classical.

'Wouldn't I give anything to take a pair of castanets into Miss Willans' class!' I said one day, 'and give a demonstration right in the middle of the Classical Mime!'

'No castanets at the Wells!' chanted June Two.

'I know!' I laughed. 'At the Russian Imperial School, et cetera! I was only *saying*.'

'How long have you been in the Junior School?' asked Valerie Makepeace, a new girl.

I considered.

'This is my sixth term,' I said at length. 'Nearly two years, and I don't think I dance a bit better than I did when I came, though Miss Hewitt said yesterday I've got quite a good chance of getting my GCE exam, so that's always something.'

Yes, Miss Hewitt's chance remark was indeed the only bright spot in a gloomy world. All my classmates, over the age of fifteen, were being moved up into the Senior School at the end of the term. I was the only one to be left behind. Miss Willan was very kind about it, merely saying that I wasn't yet up to the standard – which was true enough – and that I had better go on working in the Junior School for another term or two. But I knew in my heart that I never *would* reach the standard of technique required for that most exacting place – the Sadler's Wells Senior School.

Mariella was sympathetic when I told her about it that night.

'We seem to be both in the same boat,' she said, 'and a leaky boat at that! I've *got* to dance because of Mummy, and you – by the way, why *do* you want to dance, Caroline? I mean, why did you come to the Wells in the first place?'

'Someone asked me that at school only this morning,' I said, 'and really, it's hard to explain. I want to dance, of course, or I shouldn't have come here, but I don't want to dance the sort of things they teach you at the Wells. Honestly, Mariella, I don't really know what I *do* want.'

'Poor you!' said Mariella sympathetically. 'It must be awful not to know what you want to do. Now *I* know exactly what *I* want to do. I want to ride a pony. I want to hunt. I want to be out in the sunlight, and the wind, and the rain every second of the time. I never want to see a studio, or a *barre*, or those awful gilt mirrors, or a rosin-box ever again!' She stopped to take a breath; then went on: 'I hate walking on pavements all the time. I want to walk on dead leaves, and heather, and springy moorland turf, and pine-needles. Oh, Caroline – if I could only be *you*, or my cousin Jane. The most lovely time of my life was that summer when I stayed with Jane at Monks Hollow.'

'Well, some time you must certainly come and stay with us,' I said. 'Some time when you aren't working for an exam.'

'That'll be never!' declared Mariella gloomily, taking her point shoes out of her bag and making a naughty face at them. 'Life seems to be one dancing exam after another. But thanks, all the same, Caroline, for the kind thought. Well, I must be off to do some practice. Maestro was more sarcastic than ever about my *entrechats* this morning. He said I reminded him of the nursery rhyme: "The cow jumped over the moon" – me being the cow, of course! Why not come and practise, too, Caroline. Then we can be two old cows together!'

Chapter 2

Uncle Elmer

It was about half-term when Mariella's Uncle Elmer came to stay with us. I must tell you a little about Uncle Elmer. Of course, he wasn't my uncle, but I called him that out of courtesy, just as I called Mariella's father 'Uncle' Oscar.

Uncle Elmer was Mariella's father's brother-in-law, and he had lived in America – he called it 'the States' – nearly all his life, though he'd actually been born in London. His full name was Elmer D. Vandenhuten, and he was now having the first real holiday of his hard-working life. What his work in America was I couldn't quite make out, but it was obvious that it was some real, he-man job, out in the open air, and that he worked hard. No one who didn't work hard in the open air could have been such a splendid figure of a man as was Uncle Elmer. He was six feet four inches tall, with broad shoulders and slender hips, and his face was the colour of mahogany. His eyes were intensely blue, with a far-away expression, as if he were used to looking long distances. He talked slowly and deliberately with a rich drawl.

I must also describe Uncle Elmer's clothes, because they weren't in the least ordinary. He usually wore a cream-coloured linen suit, with a broad-brimmed panama hat, and large tan suede shoes with white-kid strapping. When he strode down the Strand, everyone turned round and stared at him, not because of his queer clothes – Londoners are so used to people in strange garments, they're not astonished at anything – but because of his height and general splendour. I may add that in Newcastle he would have had a crowd round him in no time, thinking he'd come out of the nearest circus, and demanding his autograph!

As for Uncle Elmer, himself, I'm sure he would have been more surprised than anybody if you'd told him he was the least bit unusual. He would have remarked that 'way back home' there were 'plenty of guys just like me. Yes, sir!' He'd saved up his money, and he was 'sure going to make the most of it'. He was going to take Great Britain in his stride. London he referred to as his 'home town'. After he'd seen the sights of London (the Tower, Buckingham Palace, Madame Tussaud's, and Piccadilly Circus), he was going to motor up the Great North Road in what he called his 'convertible', and take a look at Durham Cathedral for the principal reason that he'd been told 'folk kept their hosses in it'. I explained that it was quite a long time ago since the custom had been practised – in fact, not since the Scots used to raid England from across the Border. Uncle Elmer merely tilted his broad-brimmed panama hat farther over his eyes, and remarked that: 'It sure was a cute idea!'

After he'd taken his 'look' at Durham, Uncle Elmer was going on to North Shields, mainly because someone 'way back across the herring-pond' (meaning the Atlantic Ocean) had a grandmother who lived in a small back street in a poor part of the town, and he had a message to deliver to her 'personally', he added, rolling his r's. Nothing and nobody could divert him from this purpose, though it was quite a bit out of his way. He had a heart of gold, had Uncle Elmer.

After the grandmother had been seen, he was going to 'do' Hadrian's Wall, and then he intended to pay Edinburgh a visit, taking Melrose Abbey, and several other ancient monuments in his stride. He wanted to see Princes Street, Edinburgh Castle, the Royal Mile, and the Palace of Holyroodhouse – he was as fond of royalty as are most Americans! He'd left a whole day for the 'doing' of Edinburgh.

Leaving the Scottish capital, Uncle Elmer was going on to the Scottish Highlands. First, the Pass of Glencoe, then (consulting what he called his 'i-tinary') the island of Skye, which he had read was a favourite with Bonny Prince Charlie. He proudly stated that he had allowed two whole days for Skye. In vain Mariella and I tried to explain to him that, although Skye was not so big as islands go, yet its coastline was so indented by sea lochs that it was nearly a thousand miles long. He replied that he'd got it all fixed on the 'i-tinary'. He reckoned the old car (this year's model) could cover one thousand miles in a couple of days – if you stepped on the gas!

Well, I'd been on a visit to Skye with Mummy the summer before last, and I'm afraid I couldn't help laughing at the thought of Uncle Elmer in his white suit and panama hat cruising round and round Skye's endless, mist-enshrouded lochs in his glittering chromium-plated roadster, and grinding up and down the island's narrow, twisting mountain roads, occasionally (very occasionally) catching tantalizing glimpses of the elusive Cuillin Hills, if he was lucky!

'Yes – if he happens to hit on the one fine day a month they get in Skye!' commented Mariella, who had been there, too, though not when I had. 'But never mind, it won't worry Uncle Elmer. He'll look it all up in the guidebook, and go back home full of all the wonderful things he "saw" in Skye!'

Mariella was really very fond of Uncle Elmer. For one thing, he loved horses – a sure passport to Mariella's affections! – and for another, he loaded her with expensive presents. These ranged from a portable wireless set – 'radio' he called it – small enough to go in her pocket, to a tiny platinum bracelet watch with a dial no bigger than Mariella's thumbnail. The first present he'd given her was an enormous box of 'candy', tied round with a large pink satin bow, which Mariella used as a sash for her nightie. Unfortunately, Mariella couldn't eat the 'candy' because her mother said American confectionery was terribly fattening, and neither could I for the same reason.

'What do you suppose he thinks I'm going to do with *this*?' Mariella said one morning, about a fortnight after he had come to stay with us. 'This' was an almost life-size doll, dressed in satin and brocade like a lady out of a Turkish harem. It really looked most exotic, sitting on Mariella's bed, its wonderful dress spread out in glittering folds, its spun-gold hair glistening through its eye-veil, its pointed Turkish slippers, turned up at the ends, looking like something out of the *Arabian Nights*. 'I'm not supposed to *play* with it, am I?'

'Oh, I don't think so!' I laughed. 'I think that in America grown-up people have them in their bedrooms or boudoirs just for ornaments. I don't think it's meant to *play* with!'

'What a blessing!' said Mariella with a sigh of relief. 'I always hated playing with dolls, even when I was a kid. And I certainly couldn't imagine anyone playing with this one.' She gave it an awestruck glance. 'It would be like playing with the Queen of Sheba, or somebody. I can see she despises me! . . . Oh, gosh! Don't say it's nine o'clock already! Why have I got to do lessons when you have a half-term holiday?'

'You had a half-term holiday last week,' I reminded her.

'Oh, did I? I believe you're right. I'd forgotten. It seems an awful long way away!'

Mariella's lessons must have been a positive nightmare to her tutors. Perhaps it was due to her red hair, or perhaps she was a little spoilt; anyway, she certainly led her governess, Miss Linton, an awful dance. Some days she was as good as an angel, and then Miss Linton would lose her harassed expression, and manage to instil quite a lot of knowledge into Mariella's red-gold head. But at other times, Mariella was what Uncle Elmer called – no, I won't tell you what he called her, because it was something very rude!

Miss Linton had a very high-sounding name. It was Honoria Linton, MA (Hons), Cantab, but in spite of the letters after her name she really wasn't any good at dealing with her high-spirited pupil. She rather reminded me of a sheet of tissue paper trying to hold up a ninety-mile-an-hour gale! Mariella drew faces in her exercise books, and played Noughts and Crosses on the blackboard, and sometimes she had a point-to-point race meeting across her desk, with her pencils for hurdles, and her indiarubber for her favourite horse. It certainly jumped marvellously when you bent it in the middle! But really, it was no wonder Uncle Elmer called her a little you-know-what!

Mariella had two people to teach her. Besides Miss Linton, there was a meek little man called Osbert Darlington, MA (Oxon), whom Mariella called 'Ozzy' for short. Ozzy didn't come to the flat every day, though, like Honoria, but only on Tuesdays and Thursdays.

On the particular day I'm talking about, Mariella was in one of her bad moods. I think it may have been due to the fact that she'd had her half-term holiday, while mine was still to come. Anyhow, it was quite clear to everyone that Mariella was going to be 'difficult'.

'Oh, hullo, Hon!' she called from her bedroom. 'I'm afraid I'm going to be late for lessons this morning. You see, I've got the most awful rheumatism in my legs, and it's going to take me at least half an hour to walk into the schoolroom.' The 'schoolroom' was one end of the lounge which had been furnished with a small table, two chairs, and a couple of bookcases, one of which held textbooks, and the other classics that Miss Linton hopefully thought Mariella might be tempted to read.

'As if I'd read *that* stuff!' Mariella had said to me shortly after I'd come to stay with her. 'Why, they're all dreary stories about people who die, and poetry, and things! Now, if there were some stories about horses—'

But to get back to the day in question. Of course, Mariella hadn't got rheumatism, or anything at all the matter with her. Why, only half an hour before her governess' arrival she'd been pretending to jump a five-barred gate with the help of the back of the settee for a mount, and a couple of cushions for a saddle. Besides, who ever heard of a dancer suffering from rheumatism? But of course old Honoria was taken in.

'Mariella! My poor child! Has the doctor been sent for?' She came fussing into her pupil's bedroom like an old hen, as Mariella said afterwards. 'Mariella! Where are you?'

There was a chuckle from the top of the wardrobe.

'I'm up here, darling!' said naughty Mariella. 'And I can't for the life of me think how I'm going to get down again – not with my rheumatism! Perhaps we'd better have our ancient history lesson with me up here. We can pretend I'm sitting on top of a Greek temple, or something!'

Miss Linton began to see that Mariella was making fun of her.

'Mariella!' she said as severely as she knew how, which was about as severe as a little grey mouse, 'Mariella, come down this minute!'

'Shan't!' said Mariella with a toss of her bright curls. 'Go and read your beastly ancient history to yourself! I don't feel like the gloomy Greeks and Romans today!'

'But think of your poor father,' said the distracted Miss Linton. 'He's paying me to teach you.'

'Then, aren't you lucky!' retorted Mariella. 'You'll get paid all for nothing this morning. And now, this is *my* bedroom, I'll remind you, and I don't like people sitting about in my bedroom. So, please get out!' She threw a well-aimed sponge at the unfortunate Miss Linton. It was a very wet sponge, and it hit a bull's-eye.

'Oh, Mariella! Look what you've done!' cried Miss Linton, mopping her dripping bosom. 'How very naughty! How unkind!'

'Well, I told you to get out, didn't I?' said Mariella. 'So, be off with you quickly before I throw the soap at you, too! And I've got a jar of bath salts up here, as well. It will make an awful mess on the carpet – like hailstones! I give you just three minutes to *scram*, as Uncle Elmer would say. *Get out!*'

'And this,' said a voice in a well-known American drawl, 'this is where *I* come in!'

'Oh, hullo, Uncle Elmer!' said Mariella, brightening up. 'Oh, Uncle Elmer! . . . What are you doing?'

'I'm going to do what I've been itching to do almost every day since I came back home!' said Uncle Elmer, reaching for

Mariella's hairbrush. 'I'm going to apply *this* to someone where it hurts most! Yes, sir!' He reached up a long, strong arm and plucked Mariella off the top of the wardrobe as if she were a kitten.

'Oh, stop, Uncle Elmer!' yelled Mariella. '*Stop it!* Modern girls don't get spanked! English girls don't – ow!'

'But you see, Mariella, you've forgotten something! I'm not English. I'm one hundred-per-cent American, and in this particular instance I'm not too sure whether I'm really modern either!'

After a few minutes Mariella stopped yelling, and Uncle Elmer stopped whacking, and I stopped laughing. Although I know I shouldn't have laughed, I just couldn't help it. As for Honoria Linton, she was running round Mariella like a hen who's lost her one-and-only chick.

'Oh, Mariella, my dear – how very unfortunate!' she kept on saying, and whether she meant Mariella's naughtiness or Uncle Elmer's spanking I don't know!

'Take it easy, lady!' said Uncle Elmer, letting Mariella go and shooing Miss Linton into an easy chair. 'You sure have let this kid get away with too much. She's a nice kid, but you've got to show her who's boss' – he pronounced it 'borce'. 'Once you've done that, she'll eat out of your hand.'

It was all very well for Uncle Elmer to talk! It wasn't hard to imagine *him* as a person's 'borce', but poor Honoria Linton – I'm afraid I began to laugh again. As for Mariella, she began to laugh, too, though she was distinctly scarlet in the face by this time. I must say this for Mariella – she never sulked. She didn't bear Uncle Elmer any grudge, either, and I really think she was more polite to Miss Linton than hitherto. She certainly was when Uncle Elmer was about, anyway!

Chapter 3

We Go to a Concert

IT was a week or so after this, and near the end of term, that Uncle Elmer took Mariella and me to the concert. It was to be held in the sun pavilion of the roof-garden of a well-known London store. The proceeds were for charity, and the gardens were to be illuminated, so Mariella told me.

'Mummy's dancing at it,' she added. 'They always have a few celebrities at these things, and she's the chief one. It'll be frightfully boring – the concert, I mean – but the gardens will be fun. You've never seen Derry and Toms' roof-gardens, have you, Caroline?'

'No,' I answered. 'How can you have a garden big enough for a concert on the top of a roof? I suppose you mean a sort of flat roof, with things growing in tubs – like your veranda?'

'Oh, no!' said Mariella. 'They're not like that a bit. They're real gardens, with trees and paths, and even a little waterfall. I think these particular roof-gardens are the only lovely things in London!'

'Oh, Mariella!' I said shocked. 'What about all the art galleries?'

'You talk just like Mummy!' laughed Mariella. ' "My dear, what about the theatres, and the shops, and the Tate Gallery? What about Bond Street, and the Mall, and Leicester Square in the spring, and Covent Garden Opera House? You can't hate *all* London. *Quelle drôle idée!*" But you see, *I do*,' affirmed Mariella. 'I'd exchange all smelly old London, with its beastly theatres and shops, for one nice, clean, stable smelling of honest-to-goodness horse! But these roof-gardens – well, you can hardly believe they're London at all – all that way up above the streets—'

Mariella made me so curious, going on and on, talking of the wonders of the roof-gardens, that I could hardly wait until evening came on the day of the concert. As we went up in the lift through the closed store, I thought how different Derry and Toms looked at night, its floors empty and silent, all the plaster models shrouded in dust-sheets, from the way the great shop looked during the day, with crowds and crowds of people surging about everywhere. It was like passing through a sleeping city, or the palace full of enchanted people in the ballet *The Sleeping Beauty*. I mentioned the fact to Mariella, but all she said was: 'Oh, yes, I suppose it does look funny, all shut up. I've never thought of that before. Look, Caroline, there's a notice of that film with the wonderful horse in it – you know, the one who's supposed to understand every word you say to it. Oh, I wish we could go and see it. But it's *miles* away – at Putney – and I have a beastly dancing class tomorrow night. I wonder if I dare skip it?'

Fortunately, just at this moment, we arrived at the top floor, the lift stopped, and we had to get out. Mariella forgot all about the horse and the film, and began to explain about the roof-gardens.

'There's only two feet of soil,' she told me, 'so really it's rather wonderful to see quite big trees growing up here, hundreds of feet above the street.'

'Oh, and look at the waterfall!' I exclaimed. 'And a pond with real ducks on it!'

'Yes, and all the water comes from artesian wells,' said Mariella knowledgeably. 'So the London Water Board can't grumble! I told you this place was fun, didn't I? If only it wasn't for their mouldy concert, and all these dismal people—'

'Sh! Mariella!' I warned her. 'They'll hear you.'

'Don't care if they do,' said Mariella, but she lowered her voice. To do her justice, she never hurt people intentionally. She was really a very kind girl at heart.

'Think how lovely it would be up here at night – just us, and nobody to say : "Excuse me, please – may I pass!" and

"Can you tell me the way out, please, little girl."' Wickedly Mariella mimicked the sightseeing public.

'I'm sure they don't really talk like that!' I giggled.

'Oh, yes, they do – some of them, anyway,' insisted Mariella. 'You just notice! Well, as I was saying before you interrupted me, wouldn't it be lovely up here all by ourselves—cool, and dewy, and scented?—'

'And then we'd look over the parapet and see all the lights of London far below!' I said, thrilled at the thought.

'Oh, Caroline! You *would* go thinking of something like that!' said Mariella in disgust. 'Just when I was trying to forget about mouldy old London, you go and remind me of it! I was trying to imagine myself in the *real* country.'

As Mariella had prophesied, some people did approach us. They didn't ask us to excuse them, nor did they inquire the way out. They hailed Mariella as an old friend. After making a face behind Uncle Elmer's back, Mariella made the introductions. She had certainly been taught lovely manners by someone – whether by her mother, or her father, or Miss Linton, I never knew, but it was a fact, she was never at a loss.

While they were talking I slipped away to explore a little before the concert began. I sat down at length on the edge of a lily-pond, and thought how lovely the trees looked, their branches hung with hundreds of fairylights, many of which were reflected in the water beneath them. A fish with gleaming golden scales swam languorously from underneath a lily-pad, then came to the surface and stared fixedly at the lights in the trees above as if hypnotized. He reminded me of the time they'd caught men poaching salmon from the stream at Bychester Tower, where Nigel Monkhouse lived. Sebastian had told me how the poachers held lights over the stream, and the fish had swum towards them, half out of curiosity, half hypnotized.

'Stupid, silly things!' Sebastian had exclaimed.

'Oh, I don't know,' I said aloud. 'After all, they're only fish.'

'I agree!' said a voice from the shadows behind me – a well-known, mocking voice. 'And mighty queer fish, too, some of them – the people here, I mean!'

Of course I jumped, and the programme I'd been holding on my lap fell into the pool, frightening the fish, which vanished like a flash of living fire.

'Oh, Sebastian! It can't – it can't really be you, Sebastian! Why, you're in – in the place with the funny name!'

'Leipzig,' said Sebastian, coming out from the shadows and sitting down beside me. '"The prisoner," as it says in the hymn, "has leapt to lose his chains!" In other words, I'm on holiday for a week, so I came back to see how you all were.'

'But to meet you here!' I exclaimed. 'I just can't believe it! I never expected you to be on a roof-garden, of all places.'

'Don't you know that the celebrated Irma Foster is dancing her famous Dance of the Phoenix. Couldn't miss that, now could I?'

'I don't believe you care all that much about Irma Foster and her dancing,' I teased. 'I believe there's another reason for your being here. Come clean, Sebastian!'

'Well, yes, there is,' he admitted. 'If you'd looked at your programme, instead of throwing it to the fishes, you'd have seen what it was. But it's too late, now, I'm afraid.' He nodded towards the sodden, pulpy mass that had once been my programme. 'Never mind – you'll find out all in good time.'

'You don't mean – you can't possibly mean you're going to perform yourself?' I said, a sudden light dawning upon me.

'Guilty!' said Sebastian with a grin. 'But that's only one reason for my presence in this illustrious spot tonight, and believe me, it cost me wire-pulling in plenty to be allowed to perform. If it hadn't been for Monsieur X being a lifelong friend of Madame Y, who knew Mr Z, these roof-gardens wouldn't have seen even the shadow of a ghost of your humble servant.'

'But the other reason?' I prompted.

'Have patience, dearest Cousin Caroline,' said Sebastian.

'Patience, you know, is the greatest of all virtues – or is it Charity. I always forget.'

He made me a sweeping bow, and left me. Although he looked older and thinner, he was just the same mocking, sarcastic, maddeningly provoking Sebastian!

I got up from my seat by the lily-pond, and went over to the terrace, or sun pavilion, where the concert was to be held. All the chairs were taken, and I couldn't find Mariella or Uncle Elmer anywhere. I perched myself on the end of a green-painted tub filled with pink geraniums, and strove to obey Sebastian's orders, and to be patient.

The concert seemed to me to be a very good one. There were several well-known singers, BBC entertainers, and more than one television *artiste*. Near the beginning were two famous people who came straight from their act on the stage of a big London vaudeville theatre, and who appeared 'by kind permission'. I hardly heard or saw them. All the time I was waiting breathlessly for Sebastian to appear. When at last he came and sat down at the piano I could hardly conceal my excitement. His closely cropped dark head remained bent for a moment or two as if in thought; then the air was filled with the notes of Schumann's lovely *Carnival Suite*. I had heard Myra Hess play it; I had heard Eileen Joyce. Of course, I was probably quite wrong, but I liked Sebastian's rendering best. I was so proud to think that I knew, had grown up with, the young man who was holding spellbound that critical London audience. I wanted to get up and shout: 'I'm Sebastian's cousin! I used to ride with him on the moors! I live in his ancestral home!'

Some people sitting near me must have noticed how thrilled I was, for they turned round and smiled at me. I expect they thought it was Sebastian's playing that had moved me, and so, of course, it had. But there were other things too. When the last lovely note had died away, I couldn't resisting bending over towards them and whispering: 'Sebastian Scott is my cousin, you know.'

'Oh, is he, indeed?' said the lady. 'How interesting! He's a very talented young man, I think. You must be proud of him.'

With a shock I realized that Sebastian was what she had just said – no longer a boy, but a young man of twenty. To me he didn't seem a day older than he had been when we'd ridden and played together at Bracken Hall.

'And this other young man – do you know him, too?' asked the strange lady.

I looked up, and at the same moment a well-known sound reached my ears – an exciting sound that made one think of swirling skirts and mantillas, of dark-eyed Spanish beauties, of delicate wrought-iron gates leading into mysterious, shadowy courtyards, of orange groves in old Seville – the click of the castanets!

'Angelo!' I exclaimed under my breath. 'I might have known!' 'Oh, yes,' I added, turning to answer the strange lady. 'Yes, I know Angelo very well. He's Sebastian's greatest friend, and, as a matter of fact, Angelo once asked me to dance with him – to be his partner, I mean.'

'Oh, then you're a dancer?' said the lady with interest.

'Yes, I'm at the Wells School,' I told her. 'But I'm not very good – not at ballet, I mean; and, unfortunately, they don't do Spanish dancing at the Wells – not real Spanish. There are no castanets at the Wells!'

I don't know whether the lady believed me, but I didn't care. I was far too engrossed in watching the well-known slender figure of my childhood friend. He was older, too, of course; but you didn't notice it until he turned with his profile against the light. Then you saw that he, also, was a young man and not a boy any longer.

Then I became aware of Angelo's partner. I had borrowed a programme from the friendly lady, and in it I saw: Angelo Ibañez and Margarita Gitana. Margarita was a lovely, slender girl of about seventeen, with flashing dark eyes and piquant features. I guessed that she was the 'Marjorie' who had danced with Angelo at Lady Blantosh's concert years ago. If so, then she was no more Spanish than I was! I couldn't help being the tiniest bit jealous of her!

They danced beautifully together, accompanied by three guitarists. The plaintive, even sad, notes of the instruments made an effective background for stamping feet, swirling skirts, and the rhythmical clicking of the castanets. I could hardly wait till the end of the concert so that I could tell them how lovely I thought them. I longed more than anything to see and speak to Angelo. Alas, I was doomed to disappointment.

'Oh, Caroline—' It was Sebastian at my elbow. 'Did you enjoy the show? Angelo asked to be remembered to you, and he and Margarita wished to make their apologies. They had to leave before the end. They're booked to dance at some ball or other. Angelo said he was most disappointed not to see you.'

'I'm disappointed, too,' I answered. 'I was looking forward to meeting him again. It seems ages since I had a real talk to Angelo. But now I know he's in London, perhaps we shall be able to meet.'

Sebastian smiled.

'Perhaps – if you're very quick about it. But he's off to Spain in a week or so. He has a contract to dance for six weeks with a Spanish company. It will be a great experience for him.'

'And what about his partner, Margarita?' I asked.

Sebastian's brow puckered.

'She's a bit of a mystery, that girl. She won't say she's going with him, and she won't say she isn't. Can't make her out. Of course, she's only a kid, like you – seventeen or so – but she's old enough to make up her own mind, and not keep Angelo hanging about waiting for her to decide what she's going to do, or not going to do.'

'Oh, well – I expect she'll decide in her own good time,' I answered. To tell you the truth, I wasn't very interested in Angelo's girl partner. 'I wonder where Mariella and Uncle Elmer can have got to?'

'You mean the kid you stay with – girl with red hair?' Sebastian said. 'Isn't that her talking to the large-size lady? And I expect that's Uncle Elmer with the outsize in brown shoes. He looks like an "Elmer"! American to the core! Am I wrong, lady?' Sebastian mimicked Uncle Elmer's drawl so wonderfully that I burst out laughing.

'Yes, that's Uncle Elmer,' I said. 'He's a dear, even if he does wear funny clothes. He calls that tartan bow tie he's wearing "cute"!'

'I expect he thinks *your* clothes are just as funny,' commented Sebastian. 'Aren't you just typically British, Caroline! Anything anybody else wears is "funny"!'

'Well, you needn't be so superior,' I said haughtily. 'Just because you've travelled abroad for a few weeks.'

'Months,' corrected Sebastian solemnly. 'Come on, Caroline. Let's look at the lights. Your friend Mariella and her American uncle evidently haven't missed you.'

He took my arm and drew me over to the parapet on the side of the garden opposite the sun pavilion. 'I think this is the only way London looks at all presentable.'

'You sound like Mariella!' I laughed. 'She hates London. She says she'd rather live in a stable than in Buckingham Palace!'

'She sounds sensible-like, as they'd say in "canny Newcastle",' declared Sebastian. 'I agree entirely. But, of course, one's got to come to London to study. See that blaze of light over there. That'll be Piccadilly Circus, and farther over Oxford Circus, and after that Leicester Square. Imagine them all at this minute, seething with theatre crowds! Funny – it's as quiet up here as if there wasn't a theatre crowd within a hundred miles of us. If we stay much longer, we'll have the garden to yourselves. Just us – and a coupla ducks, as they say in Yorkshire!'

'And a few London sparrows,' I added. 'You mustn't forget *them*! Oh, and a blackbird and his mate. Someone told me they nest here every year. Poor darlings! They must lead a disturbed life! Just when it's time for all decent birds to go to bed, some idiotic human beings turn up and begin singing and dancing. All the lights flash on – even under the bushes, and up in the trees. Certainly no place for a home-loving couple to rear a family. No wonder Miss Bessie Blackbird leaves the nest at an early age, and goes on the spree!'

'By the way,' said Sebastian, leaning his arms on the stone coping and looking down into Kensington High Street far below, 'by the way, Caroline, do you ever see Veronica?'

For a moment I was so surprised at his mentioning Veronica that I didn't answer. Then I shook my head.

'Oh, no. I thought I told you, Sebastian – Veronica doesn't know I'm here.'

'Yes, of course, I knew that, but what I really meant was had you seen her dance?'

'I only saw her once,' I said. 'Mariella and I went to Sadler's Wells Theatre, and saw her in *Sylphides*, but somehow it seemed all wrong to see Veronica in the *corps de ballet*. And by the way, we saw *you* that night, too, Sebastian – in the foyer – but you went hareing off, and we couldn't catch you. Anyone would think you were winning the Derby!'

'Sorry!' apologized Sebastian. 'You should have yelled.'

'We did.'

'Oh, then I must have been thinking hard. When I'm doing that I never see my friends. They're used to it by now! But I know what you mean, Caroline, about Veronica being in the *corps de ballet*. Not that there's anything wrong with being in the *corps de ballet*, of course – everyone's got to be in it at first. But as you say – not Veronica!' He paused, then went on: 'As a matter of fact, you won't see Veronica in the *corps de ballet* any more, Caroline. She's been getting solo parts for quite a bit now. Between you and me, I've seen her dance a lot lately – without her knowing, of course. Besides seeing her here before I went to Leipzig, I saw her afterwards in Lisbon, and again in Paris during the Christmas holidays. I have an idea she's going to be given a chance to dance something big at

Covent Garden before long. It'll be a matinée, I expect. When that happens, and if she makes the grade, it'll mean she'll jion the Big Five.'

'The Big Five?' I echoed.

'Yes. Haven't you heard of the Big Five? Fonteyn, Shearer, Elvin, May, and Gray,' rattled off Sebastian. 'After that it'll be a case of the Little Nigger Boys, only in reverse. "Up danced another one, and then they were six!" ... Oh, I know what you're thinking, Caroline. You're wondering about my quarrel with Veronica. It was a very long time ago, that quarrel. I'm wiser now.'

'You mean – you really mean – you're going to make it up with her?' I said, unable to believe my own ears.

'I'm not going to apologize to her, if that's what you mean,' said Sebastian, sticking out his chin, 'because I still consider she treated me shamefully. But I don't mind burying the hatchet, and letting bygones be bygones.' He was silent for a few minutes, then went on half to himself: 'I did think of sending her some red roses – as a peace offering.'

'Oh, what a lovely idea!' I exclaimed. 'Veronica will love them. She adores roses – especially the dark red velvety ones. When will you send them, Sebastian?'

'When she appears in a really important role,' he answered. 'That may be any time now, as I said before. She's dancing at Covent Garden tomorrow night, you know, in *The Gods Go A-Begging*, and she's the Serving Maid. But I don't call *that* a really big role. I shall be there, of course, but not in evidence.'

'It's funny,' I said, 'but that time I told you about, when Mariella and I saw Veronica at Sadler's Wells, she was in *The Gods Go A-Begging* then, too. She was one of the Black Lackeys—'

'And now she dances the principal role,' finished off Sebastian. 'That's ballet for you! Small profits, quick returns, as the multiple shops say!'

'It only *seems* quick to the outsider,' I told him. 'Think of the years and years of gruelling work before you can even appear as a Black Lackey.'

'You *would* think of that!' teased Sebastian. 'As for me, I prefer to think of a dancer as a shooting star.'

'But shooting stars come down – not up,' I argued.

'Do they? I hadn't noticed. Well, I dare say you're right. And I dare say that applies to dancers, too – more come down than go up!-

'Yes – I'm quite sure you're right,' I said soberly.

Sebastian turned to me in surprise.

'Why, Caroline, what's up? You said that as if you meant it.'

Suddenly I felt I must tell someone about everything.

'Oh, Sebastian,' I blurted out, 'I'm a ghastly failure! I can't dance for toffee! I'm just awful! I can't get the proper "turned-out" position, and when I try to get it I go all strained, which is almost worse! And I haven't the necessary sense of "line" for classical ballet, I haven't the balance, I haven't *anything*! I don't even enjoy dancing any more. Oh, Sebastian – I wish I'd never heard about ballet! I wish – oh, you don't know how much I wish – I'd never come to the Wells!'

'Poor old Caroline!' said Sebastian tenderly, turning his back diplomatically, whilst I wiped away a large tear that persisted in trickling down my nose. 'But you mustn't say that. You know what my father says?'

'W-what does he say?' I asked miserably.

'He says one must never count the game lost or won until the last counter has been played. Wise old bird, my father!'

'It's a lovely idea,' I said, licking away another tear, 'but I feel in my case the last counter *has* been played.'

'One's last counter can't be played – at fifteen,' said Sebastian from the wisdom of twenty. 'So cheer up, Caroline. Listen – I'll tell you something I wouldn't tell another living soul – not even the blackbird that's obviously asking for my attention! I'm going to become engaged to Veronica – if she'll have me. Look!' He dug deep into his pocket and produced a tiny heart-shaped leather case, and turned his electric torch upon it – the fairylights had all been turned off by this time, and the garden was in shadow.

'Oh, Sebastian!' I breathed. 'How lovely! A ring!'

'Yes – it's a very old one, too,' he told me. 'It's been in the Scott Family for hundreds of years. It's what you call a posy-ring. Inside it, you see, is the "posy" – the word *Mizpah*, which means, "God watch between thee and me". Well, there's been no one for me but Veronica ever since the very first day I saw her funny little pale face in the Flying Scotsman. She was feeling sick, so you see it's not always romance that begets romance!'

'What stones are they?' I asked taking the ring on the palm of my hand.

'Rubies, emerald, sapphires, and the big one in the middle is a fire-opal,' he said. 'Well, we'd better be getting along, or we'll be getting shut in here for the night. If I'm not much mistaken, your friends are coming this way. Bye, Caroline!' He dropped the tiny box into his pocket, and was gone like a shadow. Really, it was hard to believe he'd been there at all!

'Oh, hullo, Caroline! We wondered where on earth you'd disappeared to!' called out Mariella, as she came towards me, her arm linked through that of her Uncle Elmer. 'How did you like the concert? Mouldy, wasn't it?'

'Oh, I thought it was *beautiful*,' I answered, thinking of Sebastian's rendering of Schumann, and Angelo's dancing.

'It's a good thing we don't all like the same things,' said Mariella with a shrug. 'The only bit I liked was that man who gave a humorous recitation about a race meeting. Anyway, it wasn't high-brow, and there were quite a lot of funny bits in it about horses. I must remember to tell Jane, when I write to her. Mummy was in good form tonight, wasn't she? She's supposed to have given up dancing, you know, but of course she never does. Uncle and I tried to congratulate her on her performance, like good relatives should, but we couldn't get near her. Balletomanes hemming her in, six deep!' Mariella made a little *moue* of disgust with her lips. 'In any case, she's going on to a supper party at the Ritz. Some rich American – like you, Uncle Elmer, only richer – is throwing it. Come on, Caroline – they're locking this place up now, and I'm famished. Even if we can't dine at the Ritz on iced melon and caviare, there'll be coffee and sandwiches waiting for us at home.'

Chapter 4

I Feel that the Last Counter Has Been Played

It was the day before we broke up that the blow fell. You'd have thought I'd have had some warning of it – that I'd have felt a sense of impending disaster, but I didn't. In fact, after seeing Sebastian and Angelo again at the Celebrity Concert, I felt almost cheerful. So when I came out of the Director's office on that awful morning, I felt rather like a man who's been shot in the back when he least expected it.

I must have looked queer when I walked back to the dressing-room and collapsed on to a bench beside the door, because Marion saw at once there was something the matter.

'Whatever's up, Caroline?' she exclaimed. 'You look as if you'd seen a ghost!'

'So I have!' I answered, wishing I didn't feel so sick. 'Only unlike a ghost, this phantom won't vanish with the dawn! Oh, Marion, this is my very last day at the Wells.'

'W-what?'

'Yes, it is,' I repeated. 'Oh, of course, I *could* come back here next term, I suppose, and go on doing lessons in the school. I haven't been expelled at a minute's notice, or anything. But as far as my dancing goes, there's no chance – no chance at all – of my ever getting into the Senior School. The Director's just told me so. Of course, he was ever so nice about it, but, as he said, it's no use my going on hoping and hoping that I shall ever be good enough, because I never shall. Oh, I knew it, really, all along, but somehow it's awful to be told so.'

'Has he told your people yet?' said June, sitting on the floor with her tights half off and half on.

I shook my head miserably.

'No. As he said, he could have told them first, and let them break it to me – which would have been a lot easier for him – but he preferred to tell me himself, seeing that I'm fifteen and nearly grown up. I'm glad he didn't write home, because Mummy's had flu, you know, and she's been quite ill. I'm sure a shock like that wouldn't have been good for her. I asked him – the Director, I mean – if he could possibly wait for a few days before he wrote to my parents, so that I could tell Mummy myself. He said I was a k-kind little g-girl!' The memory of the Director's words made my tears overflow.

'Oh, Caroline – don't cry,' said Marion. 'I know it's awful, but it might be a lot worse. You *have* got a lovely home to go back to – not like some people. Think of Dilys Ward – she lived in a tenement with umpteen brothers and sisters, and a stepfather who drank like a fish, and knocked them about. If you were like that—'

'Oh, I know I'm lucky,' I hiccoughed. 'That's what the Director said. But I'm still most frightfully disappointed.'

'Well, it can't be helped,' said June Two, who happened to have come in and had heard the conversation. 'Marion and I are being moved into the Senior School next term, it's true, but there's nothing final about that. We may be out of it by next summer. We may have grown too tall, or too fat, or have made no progress, or *anything*. You've got to be prepared for that if you take up ballet as your career.'

As the day wore on, and the effect of the shock passed off a little, I began to think about going home. A faint ray of comfort stole into my sad heart at the thought of my lovely Northumbrian home waiting for me – even if I *wasn't* returning to it as a conquering hero. I remembered Sebastian's words: 'Never count the game lost or won until the last counter has been played.' Perhaps, I thought, perhaps this wasn't the last counter, after all.

Before going back to the flat I went to King's Cross Station and bought my ticket and a reserved seat, so as to be all ready for my long journey north the following evening.

Before I left the school the next day I looked round the empty classrooms for the last time, knowing in my heart that I would never come back there again – not as a pupil. I said goodbye to my special friends and the mistresses, and then set off down Colet Gardens towards the Underground. I was to go back to 140*a* Fortnum Mansions where tea would be waiting. My train was at five-thirty. Mariella and Uncle Elmer and I were all going to King's Cross Station together, because Uncle Elmer had changed his plans at the last moment, and now intended to 'take a look at Stratford-upon-Avon, where that wise guy, Will Shakespeare, hung out'. Mariella's father had gone to a sale of antiques at Worcester, and they were all going to meet at Stratford. After which Uncle Elmer was coming back to London to pick up his car, which was having something done to it, and was then going to progress north. Incidentally, he'd promised to spend one night at Bracken Hall on his way. Mariella was going to have a couple of dancing lessons with somebody frightfully good who lived at Stratford, and was a friend of Aunt Irma's, and after this she was coming back to London to work for her audition. As Aunt Irma had just set off for a tour of New Zealand and Australia, it looked as if poor Mariella would be pretty lonely during the summer vacation, unless, as she confided in me, she could persuade her Cousin Jane to stay with her.

We went in a taxi to King's Cross, though as a matter of fact all my luggage had already been sent off in advance, and Uncle Elmer and Mariella only had hand luggage, so we could quite easily have gone by Underground.

It was just as we were getting out at the station that I remembered something awful – I had meant to buy a small present for each of my parents, and also a souvenir for Trixie, and one for Fiona, but in the stress of the moment I'd forgotten.

'I feel dreadful about it,' I confided to Mariella. 'It was all that happening at school that put it out of my mind. Oh, what shall I do? I *can't* go home and not take them anything.'

'Afraid you'll have to,' said Mariella. 'It's too late now. What about buying them something in Newcastle, and producing it out of the depths of your suitcase later on. They'd never know.' I must have looked so horrified that Mariella added hastily: 'No, I expect it wouldn't be possible, because someone will meet you in Newcastle. Sorry not to be more helpful, but you see Uncle and I have got to get to Paddington and our train goes in half an hour. We'd like to see you into your compartment before we go.'

'You'll be OK, Caroline?' said Uncle Elmer, scooping up an armful of highly coloured illustrated papers from a nearby bookstall, and dumping them on my lap. 'Some light reading to help you while away the time till your train goes. It's not due to move off for nearly half an hour. Sorry we can't stay and keep you company. We'll have to get going! I'll be seeing you, Caroline – in Northumberland!'

'Goodbye, darling Caroline,' said Mariella. 'Do, *do* come back to the Wells next term. Think how frightfully lonely I shall be if you don't. In any case, I shall come north to see you before very long.' She gave me a great hug, and disappeared after Uncle Elmer like a small, bright butterfly in the wake of a translantic airliner. As a matter of fact, her last words came true sooner than she thought – she *did* visit Northumberland before very long. But this is quite another story.

After Mariella and her uncle had gone I made a rapid calculation. I had nearly twenty-five minutes before my train was due to move out of the station. My seat was booked. If I ran all the way I would just have time to get to a little fancy shop I knew not far from the station, buy my presents, and dash back again.

I made a careful note of the number of my seat, and also the number of the carriage, and flew down the platform like a greyhound off the leash. The ticket collector at the barrier glanced at me in that nonchalant way ticket collectors have. I expect they're used to all sorts of mad people dashing about – catching trains at the last second, finding they've forgotten their luggage or left half of it in the taxi, or the car, or the left-luggage office. Anyway, he didn't ask if the police were after me, or if I were running away from school, for which I was thankful, for I hadn't time to stop and answer silly questions.

I reached the shop in exactly seven minutes, running all the way, which wasn't bad going, considering I was carrying my suitcase – I hadn't dared to leave it in the train for fear someone stole it. It took me another five minutes to choose my presents – and I may say I've never chosen anything so quickly before in my life! – and two minutes to pay for them. This left me ten minutes before my train went – seven minutes to run back to the station, and three to spare.

I dashed out of the shop and was about to set off back the way I had come, when I saw a bus going in the right direction. I jumped on it just as it moved away from the bus stop, nearly falling flat on my nose on the platform as it moved out into the traffic stream.

'Mind your step, dearie!' yelled a fat woman, holding a large string bag, crammed to the brim, in one hand, and an orange which she was sucking loudly in the other. 'Shove along! You can squeeze in 'ere beside me!'

'Thank you!' I gasped, falling into the seat between the fat lady and a long, thin man.

'Hold tight!' yelled the conductress as we bumped along. 'Up the stairs, please! Have your fares ready! Hold tight!'

I looked round and found that the small seat between the fat woman and the thin man was the only vacant one downstairs. This was a bit of luck, and no mistake! I could nip off the bus the moment it got to my stop.

'St Pancras Station!' yelled the conductress. And a moment or two later: 'King's Cross! Over there on your left, lidy. Can't miss it! Right in front of you. Mind your step, missie! Hold tight!'

The bus zoomed away, and I shot into the dark depths of

King's Cross Station like a rabbit into its burrow when the hounds are hot on the trail, only my hounds were minutes, not dogs. The station clock said five thirty-three. I had two and a half minutes to spare!

The barrier loomed ahead of me.

My ticket! I dumped my case down upon the platform, swung round my shoulder-bag to rummage in its depths for the precious bit of pasteboard – at least, I tried to do so, but alas! there was no leather strap over my shoulder. There was nothing there at all.

I stood still, petrified. Had I left my bag in the shop? No, I couldn't have done that because I'd had it in the bus when I paid for my ticket. I remembered the large lady with the string bag and the orange. Had she helped herself to my handbag while I sat squeezed beside her in the crowded bus? Or had the bag slipped off my shoulder during my mad rush, and I hadn't noticed? I shall never know. The awful fact remained – here I was in King's Cross Station without my railway ticket. In fact, without a penny in the world except the few coppers change I had dropped into my pocket as I dashed out of the souvenir shop. And my train was due to go out any moment now! It was like an awful nightmare!

I rushed up to the barrier and tried to explain to the ticket collector what had happened. The man stared at me calmly but adamantly.

'You can't come on here without a ticket, missie,' he said firmly. 'Now stand out of the way and let the lady past.' I stood aside whilst a dark-haired girl with a cream-coloured coat slung over her shoulders dashed through on to the platform in a headlong rush to catch the northbound train – my train! She was followed by a crowd of other people – young men mostly. They hurtled towards the train like bullets out of a gun.

'But what am I to do?' I shouted wildly as soon as I could get near the man again.

'Well, if you've lorst your ticket, you've lorst it,' he declared. 'You'll have to ask your dad to get you another one, that's all.'

'But I can't! My dad – I mean my father – doesn't live here,' I argued frantically. 'He'll be waiting for me in Newcastle. Oh, can't you – *can't* you let me through? My seat's booked and everything. It's No 72, carriage B. My father will pay for me at the other end, honestly he will.'

'Can't do it, missie,' said the ticket collector. 'You should have taken better care of it. It would be as good as my job's worth to let you on to the train without a ticket. Your best plan is to tell the station-master's clerk you've lorst it, and mebbe he'll arrange it for you.'

'But there isn't another train tonight, and my people will have come all the way from B-Bracken to meet me.' My voice broke at the thought of it. 'They won't know what's happened to me when I don't turn up. I wish now I'd got a p-platform ticket, then you'd have *had* to let me through, and I'd at least have been on the train.'

'Now, miss, there's no call to talk like that,' said the ticket collector severely. 'That's a naughty thing to say, that is! You'd have been found out, you would, and sent back here just the same. Stand back, miss! The train's just going out. When it's gone, I'll take you along to the clerk's office.'

'No, you won't!' I yelled, stamping my foot. 'It's no use, now. It's too late! There isn't another train!'

'Oh, all right,' said the man huffily. 'Have it your own way. Can't do no more than offer, can I?' He clashed the barrier gate in my face and walked away down the platform, muttering things about 'spoilt kids'. He really wasn't a very understanding sort of man, but then perhaps he was tired and wanting his supper. Or perhaps he was a bachelor, with no children of his own. I expect I ought to have climbed down from my high horse, run after him, and begged him to take me to the station-master's office. Sebastian said afterwards that this is what I ought to have done, but at the time I was so furious, not only with him, but with myself for not taking better care of my bag, that it was all I could do not to burst into tears of rage, frustration, and loneliness on the spot.

I walked slowly down the platform, trying to figure out what I had better do. The only money I possessed was the few coppers jingling in my pocket, and the problem I had to solve was how to spend them to best advantage. I could ring up the Sadler's Wells School. But alas! it would be closed, now that the holidays had begun. Of course, it was possible there might be someone there – a caretaker, perhaps – but I daren't risk it. Another alternative was to ring up one of the mistresses at her private address. I went across to a row of call boxes, but alas! they were all occupied. Then someone came out of the nearest one, and I went inside. Feverishly I began to flick over the leaves of the directory. Several of the mistresses didn't seem to be on the phone – or perhaps they lived in rooms, and so their number wasn't under their own name. Miss Willan was in the book, though, so I dialled her number. There was no answer. Most likely she'd gone to a matinée and wasn't back yet, or perhaps she'd gone away altogether. I tried Miss Smailes. Someone – obviously a charwoman or a caretaker – answered my inquiry as to the whereabouts of Miss Smailes with a curt: 'Miss Smiles is out modom. She won't be in till eleven-thirty at soonest. She's gorn to the the-atre. Can I give her a message, modom?'

'Oh, no, thank you,' I answered, my hearting sinking. 'That would be much too late.'

It was only after I had put down the receiver that it occurred to me that I might have asked if I could wait in Miss Smailes' flat until that lady returned. Oh, well, I thought, now I come to think of it, I don't know how I could possibly have got all the way out to Hampstead with only three-ha'pence! The same applied to Mariella's flat. It was a long way from King's Cross Station to Fortnum Mansions, and even when I got there I still had no means of getting any money, always supposing I managed to persuade the caretaker to let me into the flat with his key. Still, this seemed to be the only thing to do under the circumstances. It was a pretty doleful thought, that walk through miles and miles of London street, with only an empty flat at the end of it. Added to this was the thought of the train – my train – speeding northwards without me, let alone the knowledge of my parents waiting anxiously for me at the other end, not knowing what had happened to me when I didn't arrive. I almost wished, now, that I hadn't stamped my foot at the grumpy ticket collector. He, together with the station-master's clerk, might have been able to suggest something. I looked through the misty glass side of the telephone box to see if he'd come back to the barrier, but he hadn't.

'Oh, dear!' I said aloud, opening the kiosk door. 'It seems to me this really *is* the last counter in the game, and I really *have* lost it.'

'Lost what?' said a voice in my ear, so close that it made me jump. 'Do I hear you say that you have lost something? Can I help you look for it?' A strange young man was holding the door open politely for me so that I could emerge. 'What was it that you have lost?'

'Oh, no, I haven't lost anything – at least not here,' I began impatiently. 'What I meant was—' I stopped abruptly. The strange young man wasn't strange at all! He was . . .

'Angelo!' I gasped. 'Angelo! You don't know how glad I am to see you!'

Angelo's dark face lit up – I couldn't help noticing that he'd been looking very tired and worried when he'd first spoken.

'And I to see you, Caroline.'

'I'm in the most awful trouble, Angelo,' I went on. 'I just don't know what to do. You see—'

'One little moment—'

He took my case from me, tucked my arm through his, and led me towards a tea-room. After he had ordered coffee and sandwiches, he turned to me again.

'Now, Caroline, *ma petite*, what is it that is the matter?'

I told him my tale of woe, and when I had finished, to my

surprise, his face broke into a smile, and his dark eyes fairly snapped with excitement.

'But Caroline, this is wonderful, *wonderful*!' he exclaimed.

'Wonderful? Whatever do you mean?' I gasped, thinking he had gone completely mad. 'How can you say that? I thought you'd be sorry for me. Why, it's the most awful thing that's ever happened to me. Think of my dancing – my career – and think of poor Mummy and Daddy waiting for me in Newcastle Station – not knowing what has become of me—'

'Oh, yes, yes – that would be bad, of course. But it is a catastrophe we must avert, yes? What time do the parents leave Bracken Hall to come to the Central Station to meet you?'

I made a rapid calculation.

'I'm not quite sure,' I said at length, 'but I know the train takes about five and a half hours, so it's due at Newcastle about eleven o'clock. It takes an hour and a half to get from Bracken to the station by car, so they'll be leaving home about half past nine. You see, I can't possibly let them know in time.'

'Oh, yes you can,' said Angelo. 'By telephone.'

'But I haven't any money,' I exclaimed. 'I've just *told* you. It was all in my bag.'

'Ah, ça!' exclaimed Angelo, snapping his fingers. 'I can let you have the money, *naturellement*.'

'Oh, no, Angelo, you couldn't possibly,' I argued. 'It's an awfully long way. A trunk call like that would cost the earth.'

'Then you can reverse the call.'

'Reverse it? Whatever do you mean?'

'I mean,' explained Angelo, 'since you refuse my offer of money, I mean that when the operator answers your ring, you can ask to have the charge reversed, so that your parents will pay it. I do not think they will object when they know the circumstances. It will save them a very long journey into town all for nothing. And also you can ring up on the cheap rate, as it is after six o'clock!'

'How wonderful!' I said. 'You think of everything! I didn't know about the reversing idea. No, of course my parents won't object. You *are* clever, Angelo! Now everything is solved.'

'Not quite everything,' said Angelo softly.

'What do you mean?' I said, startled at his tone. 'What else is there to solve?'

'Just this little puzzle of mine,' answered Angelo. 'Now drink your coffee, and I will tell you about it, for we must have it settled before you telephone your parents. It most of all concerns them.'

'What? Then it doesn't concern me?' I said.

'Ah, yes – it concerns you, of course, Caroline,' said Angelo. 'But of you I am not afraid. But of the parents – yes! And without the parents' consent, my plan he goes not! Listen, and I shall tell you about it.'

Chapter 5

I Am Led to Hope

'You have heard,' said Angelo, stirring his coffee thoughtfully, 'of my partner, Margarita?'

'Margarita Gitana?' I answered. 'Oh, yes! I saw her dance with you at the Celebrity Concert. I think she's lovely, Angelo.'

'Yes – she is very beautiful,' agreed Angelo, still stirring his coffee. 'But what you may not know is that she is not a Spanish girl at all, but an English one.'

'Yes, I knew that, too,' I said. 'Sebastian told me. If he hadn't, I'd never have guessed, though. She looks very Spanish, and I expect the dress – mantilla, and everything – makes her look more so.'

'She is not as Spanish-looking as you, Caroline,' said Angelo in that strange, soft voice that almost made me feel as if he were putting a spell upon me. 'Nor is she of so fine a character. She dance with me. She – how you say it? she lead me up a garden! "Oh, yes, Angelo," she say, "I will dance with you to the end of the world!" "So far it is not necessary," I tell her. "Only to London," I say, "to the television audition." She is thrilled at that! To appear on television – that would suit Margarita! That is one of her dreams! But now to the point. Her parents, I thought, agreed. They allow her to do what she likes. She is seventeen, eighteen,' he shrugged. 'I know not, exactly, but I know that she has left school and is old enough to dance in public. We practice together in Newcastle, and elsewhere, and then she come to London and dance with me at the Charity Concert. This is the one at which you see us! All goes well, I think, until the – how do you say it? – the balloon he goes up sky-high! I do not know that she comes to the concert without her parents' consent, and, worse than that, without their knowledge. They think all the time she stays with an aunt, while in reality she is dancing with me. Naturally a scheme like that, with the brain of a hare, cannot succeed. The good aunt is taken ill and is in a hospital, and the plan is in shreds. Margarita's father ring me up, and is very angry. It is all my fault, he says. His daughter must return home at once. She is to be a lady doctor, it seems, and not a dancer, whatever her inclinations. She is supposed to be sweating – I beg your pardon, I mean swotting – for her examination at the end of the summer. My dancing—' Angelo shrugged his shoulders expressively. 'That is of no importance to him! And, of course, I can see that it is not. But to return to Margarita – I see her to her train to Newcastle this evening. It was the same train as the one you should have travelled on. She almost missed it – my poor Margarita! she did not want to go! – and then I suppose that would have been my fault, too, but in the end we just managed to catch it!'

'Oh, I saw her!' I broke in. 'I saw you both while I was arguing with that stupid ticket collector. Margarita had a white coat on, hadn't she, and you were tearing along behind her? There were a lot of other people there, too, and I expect that was why I didn't recognize you, Angelo. I wondered why you happened to be in King's Cross Station. It seemed such a coincidence that I should meet you here, but I can see, now, that it wasn't really.'

'Oh, yes it was!' said Angelo. 'Or rather it was a stroke of Fate that led me to the very telephone box where you were making your call, Caroline. A stroke of Fate! I insist upon it!'

I hadn't the heart to tell him that all the other boxes were full. In any case, what did it matter? He was here, and that was all that concerned me.

'But why were you telephoning?' I said. 'I mean, don't you want to make your call now?'

'That can wait,' answered Angelo. 'I can do it later – when

you ring up your home. It was only to the father of Margarita that I make the call – to tell him that his daughter is really on that train. I promised to do so.' He sighed as he said this, and I knew that he had already banished the dream of himself and Margarita dancing together to fame, and had come down to earth with a bump.

'Poor Angelo!' I said softly. 'It's awful for you about Margarita. I wish I could help! But it's rather like me and the Wells. Nobody can help.'

'That is where you are wrong,' said Angelo simply. 'You can help a great deal, Caroline – if you will. You can dance with me. You can be my partner, and go with me to the audition.'

'W-what did you say?' I gasped.

'Don't you remember,' went on my companion, 'that snowy night in Northumberland when we danced at the party? I said it would come to this, did I not? I felt it in the something that is inside me that tells me of the future. But how and when it would come to pass, that, of course, I did not know.'

'But how could I possibly dance with you?' I said. 'I could dance with you, of course, but not like this – at a moment's notice. And Spanish dancing, too! I'm not trained for it. And when is the audition, anyway?'

'It is tomorrow,' said Angelo.

I stared at him, thinking for the second time that evening that he had gone mad.

'Oh, I know it sounds absurd,' said Angelo, cleverly reading my thoughts. 'And so it would be for any ordinary person, of course. But you are a highly-trained dancer, Caroline. With all that Sadler's Wells' training behind you, I could teach you in a few hours what it would take me weeks and months to teach to another person. Besides, it is only the preliminary audition tomorrow. After that there will be a camera test which may not take place for weeks. Perhaps months. After that, more months till the real performance. So you see, it is not so impossible as it seems at first.'

'Couldn't we get another preliminary audition later on?' I asked.

'I had already thought of that,' said Angelo. 'But he will not go, that plan! You see, I have a contract to dance with a company of dancers in Spain, and when I return it will be too late to get an audition for the programme for which our Spanish number is required. So you see, Caroline, it is never or now! But do not shake your head. We have all tonight, and by this time tomorrow you will be such a Spanish dancer as has never been seen before. I prophesy!'

I couldn't help smiling at his glowing enthusiasm, though I knew, of course, that the things he said couldn't come true, lovely though they sounded. I didn't yet know Angelo!

'And this is what I had to tell you before you made your telephone call,' he went on. 'I did not want to get into more boiling water with angry parents! I must ask your father and mother if they will allow you to stay and dance with me for a short time – that is, if you *want* to dance with me, Caroline.' He looked up, and his dark eyes pleaded with me.

'Of *course* I want to dance with you,' I said. 'After all, I'm no use at ballet. But, Angelo, can't you see that it's quite, quite impossible.'

'All things are possible if one is determined,' he answered. 'We have the night before us – a whole night in which to teach you, not the whole technique of the Spanish dance – that would take a lifetime – but one short Sevillanas, and to play the castanets a little.'

'As a matter of fact, I've taught myself to play the castanets quite well,' I confessed. 'It amused the girls at school, and it interested me. Of course, I didn't do it at the Wells, actually. They don't play castanets at the Wells.'

Angelo leapt up from the table, nearly upsetting the empty coffee cups, and exclaiming something in Spanish that I didn't understand. Then he went on in somewhat more sober English:

'You have nowhere to go tonight – your friend's flat is shut, you tell me, so this is indeed a godsend. I have an artist friend who lives at Chelsea. I shall take you to her studio, and we will dance and dance. When we are so tired that we drop, I shall wrap you in a black velvet robe lined with fur, that is used for the models, and you shall sleep on the models' stage, whilst I cool my hot head in the river outside the windows. Yolande will be delighted to receive you, Caroline. You must be prepared for her to sketch you as you dance – she will want to paint you, I know . . . And now for the parents . . .'

Mummy and Daddy weren't nearly as difficult as I'd feared. For one thing, a telegram had just come for me from Veronica which they'd opened, thinking it might be important. It was to say that she was dancing Odette-Odile at Covent Garden next week, and was booking seats for all of us. So, as Mummy said, it really was a blessing in disguise that I'd missed the train, because it would save me two long railway journeys and a lot of money! She supposed I *wanted* to see Veronica dance? As for Angelo's Spanish dancing, she supposed that would be all right, too. Television sounded quite respectable! And, after all, I'd gone to the Wells to dance, hadn't I? She realized that things had changed a lot since she was young, and nobody seemed to think it queer if you went on the stage. Even clergymen's children did it! She talked so long, and so fast that the three minutes were up before either Angelo or I could get a word in! When the pips had gone we put down the receiver, leaned against the telephone kiosk door, and looked at each other. Then we began to laugh.

'Poor Mummy!' I giggled. 'I don't believe she knew in the very least what I was talking about!'

'But in any case, we have her permission,' said Angelo. 'And that is the main thing. Come, Caroline – we will go to the Chelsea studio.'

As Angelo had predicted, Yolande received us with open arms. She was obviously an old friend of his, and everything she had she put at our service. Her studio was on the top floor of an old house down by the river. It was a bare place and had that air of orderly untidiness peculiar to artists. Against the wall stood a motley array of canvases, some of them river scenes, but by the far the greater number were pictures of backstage theatre life. There was a huge skylight in the attic roof, covered at the moment by a green canvas blind. The room itself was full of flickering green light, reflected on to the ceiling by the river outside. You could hear the water softly rippling against a nearby landing-stage, and now and again the sound of rowlocks came to your ears as someone passed in a boat. It was a peaceful place, and you might have imagined yourself miles and miles from London, instead of a mere twenty minutes or so from Piccadilly Circus!

Yolande, herself, was a tall, dark girl with very blue eyes and a blunt retroussé nose. Her mouth was wide and generous, and looked as if she laughed a lot, and her hair was cut in a 'page-boy' with a straight fringe across her low forehead. I thought it made her look like Trilby. She wore dark slacks and a white sweater that I suspected were old cast-offs of one of her brothers – Angelo told me she had seven of them!

I shall never forget that night! As Angelo had said, we danced until we dropped. Yolande went to bed and left us to it! When we could dance no more, I curled up on the artists' stage, and fell asleep as I was. Angelo assured me there was a summer-house in the garden where he could be quite comfortable.

'And in the morning you shall try on a costume Yolande has got for you. Goodnight, Caroline, and sleep well!'

Sleep well! I never stirred until next morning, when I was wakened by Yolande gently shaking my arm and putting down a cup of tea on the floor beside me.

We spent the morning practising the dance Angelo had taught me the night before. To my surprise, after the night's sleep, I knew it perfectly.

'I told you, did I not, that it would be easy for you,' said Angelo, looking as pleased as a dog with two tails, both wagging at once! 'You see, your Sadler's Wells' training has not been wasted, although of course many things that you did there you must now not do. You must unlearn! For example – this!' He mimicked the soft movements of my arms, changing them to the dramatic Spanish ones, fingers pointed. 'And you must no longer turn out the feet, so!'

'Thank goodness for that!' I exclaimed. 'It was the turned-out position I just couldn't manage at the Wells!'

'Well, now it is time for the costume,' said Angelo, going to a cupboard wardrobe and bringing out an armful of clothes. 'This, I think, is the dress for you. It belongs to a friend of Yolande's – a real Spanish lady—'. He tossed into my arms a dark wine-coloured dress, heavily trimmed with braid and embroidery of blue and gold. It had a wide flounce round the bottom of the skirt. 'And the petticoats' – a froth of billowy lace ruffles followed the dress. 'And lastly the black lace mittens, and the lace mantilla and comb. You will wear white stockings, and black shoes with high heels of red . . . Ah! I had almost forgotten – I have got this for your hair.' He presented me with a real carnation, dark red and scented. 'Now, if you will put these things on, I shall wait below in the garden for you.'

When he had gone, I took off my everyday skirt and jumper, and put on the clothes. As I did so, I seemed to shed the schoolgirlish Caroline, and become the romantic and fiery dancer Angelo wished me to be.

'We must find a stage name for you,' he had said before he left. 'Rosita, I think it must be, for you are beautiful and glowing as a rose!'

Of course, I knew it was only his romantic southern nature that made him say such lovely things to me, but I couldn't help turning to look at my reflection in the long mirror that hung on one wall of the studio. I gasped, for the picture I saw there told me that what he had said was true! I *was* beautiful! My arduous ballet training had made me slender and graceful, so that even my worst enemy couldn't have called me fat! My dark hair was like a cloud, shadowing my oval face, and my

To me she will always be the little girl in the cotton frock who danced with bare feet outside my window

eyes looked enormous. There was a faint shadow in them – a shadow left there by the unhappiness of the last few weeks – but this only added to their mystery.

When I had finished dressing, I went out on to the tiny iron balcony, and there below was Angelo patiently waiting for me. When he saw me, his eyes shone, and he jumped to his feet.

'You are indeed a lovely *señorita*!' he exclaimed. 'You will be a great success, Caroline. See if it is not so!'

A sudden flash of intuition seemed to come over me – perhaps I was carried away by his enthusiasm. But I knew quite certainly that what he said would come true. I *would* be a success. There would be a time when I would hold spellbound a vast London audience; a time when my name – Rosita Ibañez – would head the bills of famous theatres. Ibañez, you say? But that is Angelo's name? Yes, and mine, too! I knew, in that flash of intuition, that I was going to marry Angelo... But all that is in the dim, dim future. Just now there is work to be done...

We caught the bus to town in the early afternoon. As we crossed Piccadilly Circus, I thought of the night Mariella and I had gone there, and I had been so homesick at the sound of a Tyneside football crowd. Today I was able to smile. It's funny how you aren't homesick when you're happy. With my arm tucked through Angelo's, I walked across Piccadilly Circus as if I owned it. I felt that, although I was a ghastly failure at classical ballet, yet I was going to dance in spite of everything. Besides this, I felt that I was no longer alone. I had got a partner and a friend who, I knew, would never let me down.

Chapter 6

How Sebastian Had to Finish the Story

If anyone had told me I would turn author, quite frankly I'd have laughed in their faces. Which all goes to show that one can never be quite sure what one will turn one's hand to, should the need arise.

'No! No! No! Caroline!' I said. 'I'm a musician – not a writer!'

'Very well, then, this story will never be finished,' quoth Cousin Caroline, clicking her castanets wildly, 'because *I* haven't time to write it, and neither has Angelo, nor Veronica, nor anyone except you. Dear, dear Sebastian – you do it, *please*!'

So you see how it was that I, Sebastian Scott, came to finish the tale, the reason being that I hate things that don't end – Unfinished Symphonies, Lost Cords, and the like! So untidy! Thus the idea of Caroline's story being left unfinished just couldn't be borne – not by Yours Truly!

Well, this is how things turned out. After Veronica's first performance at Covent Garden, in a major role, we all gathered, like the Meeting of the Clans, at the Hotel Splendide to celebrate. Trust Aunt June to select the most pompous and pretentious hotel in town – red plush six inches deep on all the settees, and brass buttons two dozen to the square inch on all the page-boys, and the lifts with a distinctly snobbish drone!

Personally, I thought that my worthy aunt was looking a little the worse for wear. Perhaps it was due to the as yet unaccustomed hardship of wearing last season's hat, or perhaps last year's fur coat didn't give her the necessary aplomb (good word, that!) Anyway, she didn't ooze with money quite as loudly as before. Forgive the mixed metaphor! And, would you believe it, they actually travelled up by Pullman, third class. One wonders how they managed to endure it. All those third-class people! My dear, so *common*! Uncle John has come down a bit, too. I understand he only runs one car, nowadays. It's amazing the hardships one can undergo and yet survive!

I'm afraid I arrived a little late at the festive dinner party. That was owing to my recent engagement. Yes, Veronica decided to risk accepting me, and the hatchet is now quite buried. We have each forgiven each other! Well, after I had asked her whether she thought Veronica Scott would sound well, and we had driven away from Covent Garden, followed by the suspicious glances of several policemen who thought we were drunk – so we were, only not with liquor! – we duly arrived at dear old Mrs Crapper's lodging house. Naturally, we had to break the glad news to her, and of course she had to conduct us with due ceremony into the parlour where we were regaled with tea – tea being the panacea of all evils as far as Mrs Crapper is concerned. In her eyes, tea is the only right and proper beverage for celebrations – be they weddings or funerals!

After Veronica had changed into something worthy of dear Aunt June, we set off again for the West End, Veronica doing the signals out of the car window, and showing off her engagement ring thereby, just like any other engaged girl, bless her! She's only a kid, really – eighteen years old by the calendar, but about fifteen in actual fact!

We arrived at the Splendide at 7.10 PM and were shown (I beg your pardon, 'ushered' is the word!) up to the Scott's suite. No, it wasn't the royal one that King Somebody or Other, of some unpronounceable country, occupied in eighteen hundred of thereabouts but the one next door. Fiona came to meet us, and held out a hand plastered with diamonds. Fact! You couldn't see her for glitter!

'Oh – ho! Since when did you become a shareholder in Messrs Woolworth, Cousin Fiona?' quoth Yours Truly with a leer.

'I don't know what you mean, Sebastian,' she tittered. Yes, tittered I said, and tittered I meant. It's the only possible word for Fiona's laugh.

'You heard me!' I told her. Then we glared at each other llke a couple of cats, until Veronica stepped between us like the peacemaker she always was, and peace was restored. Veronica then kissed Fiona. Yes, actually kissed her! Really, the things women do for the sake of politeness and family feelings beat me!

Of course our news had to come out, and there were more kisses on the part of the women, and handshakes between Unclc John and me. Then right in the middle of it all, who should burst in but Caroline and Angelo. They'd just come back from the television camera test, which they'd had the unexpected good luck to secure only a few days after their successful preliminary audition. Yes, and they'd passed the test, too, so now we shall be seeing Carolinc on television!

Naturally, there were more kisses, and tears (women always cry when they're happy, I've discovered!) and congratulations. Strictly on the QT, I don't think that dear Cousin Fiona enjoyed it much. Felt her aristocratic little nose had been properly put out of joint!

'Oh, just television!' she exclaimed. 'I thought by all the fuss that you were going to appear on the *real* stage, Caroline.'

'So I am,' said Caroline. 'I've just been along to Angelo's agent, and I've been taken on with his Spanish company. So I'm going to Spain in a few days' time. Then I shall be on the *real* stage, as you call it.'

'Oh,' said Cousin Fiona, and that small word expressed all she felt.

Well, now I think the story is really finished. My fiancée, Veronica, is sitting in the window-seat of the Hotel Splendide's second-best suite, and by the remote expression on her small, pale face, I have a feeling that she has forgotten all of us, (yes, even me!) and is still being Odette in *Lac des Cygnes*. But she will never be Odette to me. To me she will always be the little girl in the cotton frock who danced with bare feet outside my window in far-off Northumberland, the little girl who confided in me her dream of being a dancer that day, long, long ago, on the Flying Scotsman.

And as for Caroline, success has come to her after all. As my father says: 'Never count the game lost or won until the last counter has been played!' That's very true, I think. Caroline has still won the game, although there were no castanets at the Wells!

If you have enjoyed this Piccolo Book, you may like to choose your next book from the titles listed on the following pages.

Other books by Lorna Hill in Piccolo

The adventures of Veronica Weston and her friends appear in the famous *Sadler's Wells* series which includes

A DREAM OF SADLER'S WELLS 20p
In this poignant yet heart-warming story Veronica proves a determined fourteen-year-old can overcome all kinds of difficulties – even to riding on horseback through the fog to catch the train for her audition.

VERONICA AT THE WELLS 20p
Veronica's ambition is to dance the Lilac Fairy at Covent Garden, but first she must gain admission to Sadler's Wells Ballet School.

MASQUERADE AT THE WELLS 20p
A daring deception is born when Mariella persuades Jane to take her place at an audition for Sadler's Wells Ballet School.

Each book is complete in itself but once you've read one story you'll want to read them all.